The Most

ALSO BY JESSICA ANTHONY

Enter the Aardvark

Chopsticks

The Convalescent

The Most

Jessica Anthony

LITTLE, BROWN AND COMPANY
New York Boston London

Copyright © 2024 by Jessica Anthony

Little, Brown and Company
Hachette Book Group
1290 Avenue of the Americas, New York, NY 10104
littlebrown.com

First Little, Brown paperback edition: July 2024

Little, Brown and Company is a division of Hachette Book Group, Inc. The Little, Brown name and logo are trademarks of Hachette Book Group, Inc.

The publisher is not responsible for websites (or their content) that are not owned by the publisher.

The Hachette Speakers Bureau provides a wide range of authors for speaking events. To find out more, go to hachettespeakersbureau.com or call (866) 376-6591.

Book interior design by Marie Mundaca

ISBN 9780316576376
LCCN 2024934366

Printing 3, 2024

LSC-C

Printed in the United States of America

To my family, and the Bridge Guards

The Most

And someday I'll know that moment divine,
when all the things you are, are mine.

—HAMMERSTEIN AND KERN

1.

Kathleen Beckett awoke feeling poorly. It was Sunday. November. Warm for this time of year. She threw off the covers and turned onto her back, undoing the bow of her sleeping gown. She wouldn't go to church, she told her husband, Virgil, but there was no need for concern. Everyone should go on without her.

Virgil hesitated. They had been going to church for six months now, and his wife had not yet missed a service. "Dear, are you sure you're all right?" he asked, flipping a necktie.

Kathleen, Kathy to her friends, Katie when Virgil felt sweet, nodded from the bed. "I'm perfectly fine," she said. "I shouldn't have slept in the flannel. You go. I'll see you when you get back."

Virgil kissed his wife on the forehead. Their sons, Nicholas and Nathaniel, were standing in the doorway. "Mother's not well," he told them. "Go dress yourselves."

The boys stared at their mother.

"What's wrong with her," said Nicholas.

Virgil glared at him. "I said your mother's not well. Don't bother her."

The boys retreated into their bedroom and put on their church suits. Virgil made breakfast, then piled everyone into the family's brand-new '57 Buick Bluebird and departed for the First Presbyterian. The church was fifteen miles from Acropolis Place, the sunny, pentagon-shaped apartment complex on the outskirts of Newark, Delaware, where the Becketts had lived since last May, ever since Virgil started at Equitable Life in Wilmington.

Kathleen had picked it out. Though it was only an apartment, it was new, carpeted in green wall-to-wall, and its signature feature was a gas fireplace that lit with a switch. There was an icebox, a floor-to-ceiling bookshelf for her novels and cookbooks. In the living room, a sliding glass door led out to a white wrought-iron balcony overlooking a small, kidney-shaped community swimming pool, which the Becketts, in their brief tenure at Acropolis Place, had never seen anyone use.

Virgil didn't care where they lived so long as Kathleen was

happy, but he'd taken a pay cut to move back to Delaware and work at Equitable. Their house in Rhode Island sold for what they paid almost a decade ago. He hoped they wouldn't stay long at the apartment.

After Christmas, he figured, they could start looking for a house in Wilmington, but until then, each Sunday the family would travel the fifteen miles to the First Presbyterian and sit in the wooden pews for forty minutes, listening to Reverend Underhill speak with passive equanimity about Jesus Christ and potluck suppers.

Usually after the service, Virgil and the other men from Equitable lingered on one part of the church's front lawn in pressed suits and fedoras, smoking and talking business, family, the free afternoon, while the women, crisp in their crinolines, lingered in the vestibule, chatting with the reverend, anticipating an afternoon of cooking and cocktails. Today, the unseasonably warm weather prompted everyone to flee the First Presbyterian as quickly as possible, leaving the reverend to watch his congregation hastily press themselves into their cars and wonder what it was he'd said that sent them running.

Virgil Beckett was the first out the door. Major chords of the last hymn still sounded in the nave as he whispered to the boys to get their coats. *I'll check on Kathleen first,* he thought. *Then I'll call Wooz.* The course was bound to be open on a day like this, though he'd never golfed this late in the season before.

There were barely any leaves on the trees.

Virgil had thought about golfing throughout the entire sermon and could not tell you a word of what Reverend Underhill said. Having grown up in California, he appreciated an Indian summer, and pictured himself in his summer shirt and slacks, swinging iron, feeling the sweat slide down his back. He imagined the smell of the warm browning grass beneath him, the sight of the hanging November sun in the sky. Now, rushing the boys to the car, he worried whether the course was actually open, and if so, whether anyone would have bothered to rake and mow.

"In you go," he said, and the boys tumbled into the back of the Bluebird.

Virgil glanced at his sons in the rearview. They hadn't spoken much this morning and were slouched in the back seat. Their coats were already off. Their faces, pink and sticky.

"You boys okay?" he said.

"We don't like church clothes," said Nicholas.

Nicholas, the younger of the two, often spoke for himself and Nathaniel.

"We're almost home," Virgil said. "When you get home you can change and then go outside. Isn't this a great day? Are you going to play stickball or something? Get a game going?"

The boys didn't answer.

Virgil struck the left-hand turn signal on the Bluebird. The car tick-tocked, and they waited.

It suddenly occurred to Virgil that Kathleen might be pregnant.

He didn't know why he hadn't thought of it until now. Though most women were finished by thirty, a third child at her age wasn't unheard of. Most of the agents at Equitable had three. But a man had to be cautious; you couldn't get greedy and take on more than you could handle. Virgil didn't know him well, but Tom Braddock had four boys and was apparently envied for years. Then, a month ago, the oldest died. It happened right outside his house. Some kind of a blockage in the brain—or was it the heart? Leg? At any rate, the boy just collapsed on the front lawn, and now Virgil regarded Braddock warily. It was the worst sort of terrible luck, he felt, the kind that might attach itself to you if you got too near it. Virgil's boss, Lou Porter, had told Braddock to take a good deal of time off, whatever he needed, and everyone pretended it was for Braddock. Truth was, no one could stand to be near him.

Virgil wondered if the baby would be a girl. It would be good for Kathy to have a girl, he thought. He was happy with his boys, but a little girl could keep Kathy company in a different way, and he worried sometimes that she was lonely in a house of men.

By the time he made the final turn into Acropolis Place and steered the Bluebird into the carport, Virgil Beckett saw the new baby girl as clearly as he saw the warm afternoon golfing. He helped the boys out of the back seat, slammed the car doors, then traveled up the stairs two at a time to apartment 14B and went directly to the bedroom to check on his wife. "Kath?" he said.

She wasn't there.

Virgil stood for a moment, looking at the bed. It was neatly made.

"Kathleen?"

He left the bedroom and searched the living room, kitchen. There was no sign of her. He was thinking she might have slipped out for some Bayer or something when he heard Nicholas cry out:

"Mother's in the pool!"

Virgil joined his sons on the balcony.

Kathleen was standing in the far end of the swimming pool, chest-deep in water, her elbows resting comfortably on the bull-nose coping. She was wearing her old red bathing suit, the one from college. He hadn't seen it in years.

"Kathy," he shouted, laughing. "What are you doing?"

The woman looked up, visoring her eyes with one hand to block the sun. A cigarette forked her fingers.

She saw Virgil and waved.

Virgil returned to the front door, traveled back downstairs, and by the time he reached the edge of the pool, a few of their neighbors had slid back their own glass doors and were standing, watching, from behind the rails of their balconies.

He knelt down. "Kath," he said. "Are you all right?"

Mrs. Beckett smiled at her husband. "I'm perfectly fine," she said. "Never felt better, in fact."

"What are you doing out here?"

Kathleen Beckett, née Lovelace, in her younger years had been an athlete. She was tall, and once slender. Her game was tennis, and she'd done well in college, winning both the '47 and '48 women's intercollegiate tournaments at the University of Delaware. A black-and-white photo of Kathleen in her tennis dress, holding her racquet, was still hanging in Memorial Library.

Her hero, she said, was Margaret Osborne duPont, the current US national champion, who by 1957 had accumulated thirty-three Grand Slam titles, ten Wightman Cups. Margaret Osborne duPont, who lived on a sprawling Wilmington estate just twenty miles northeast of Newark, had the greatest endurance of any tennis player Kathleen had ever seen. When Kathleen read in the paper that Margaret's father had died, she had written her a long letter, telling her how much she admired her.

Virgil had always liked watching Kathleen play. Her long body sailed around the court. Her right arm made a grand sweeping gesture whenever she hit the ball, and sometimes she emitted a guttural *hah!* Before graduation, Kathleen had briefly entertained the idea of playing professionally—there was a scout, Randy Roman, who would have signed her any time she wanted—but it would not have been an easy life, and Virgil was grateful that Mr. Roman had been honest about it. He explained up front what it really meant to practice all the time, to play tennis around the country—or if she won here, Australia—and in the end, Kathleen had turned him down. She graduated, married Virgil, and moved with him to Pawtucket to set up house.

After the boys were born, Kathleen continued playing tennis recreationally. She didn't always win—it was more important to give her friends a few points than beat them outright, she said, and besides, the middle part of her had never really recovered from pregnancy. She couldn't move as fast, didn't hit as hard anymore. Eventually she stopped playing tennis altogether, and now Virgil told her every day how beautiful she was.

In the pool, Kathleen lowered her forearms to the water's surface and let them float. Her brown hair was tied into a wet knot at the neck. She playfully kicked her legs, and Virgil could see the flesh on her thighs moving underwater. When her feet touched the bottom, her whole body shook, slightly.

"I was hot," she said. "That's why I came out."

Virgil stared at the blue sky and worried about Kathleen. Then he worried about the golf game. A warm November in Delaware really was a very rare thing, and he needed to call Wooz as soon as possible. Artie Wooz, the most ambitious of the fellows at Equitable, didn't wait for anyone except their boss. For Lou Porter, the men at Equitable laughed, Arthur Delano Wooz was a well of infinite patience.

It must be seventy degrees, Virgil thought, as a lingering V of Canada geese went crying over their heads. Was it noon?

"Geez, Mrs. Beckett," he said. "Haven't you cooled off yet?"

Kathleen sank, took in a mouthful of water and surfaced, spitting it out. Usually she laughed when he called her "Mrs. Beckett," but not today.

"I'm just taking a dip," she said. "We have a pool, after all, and no one uses it. When we moved here, we talked about the pool. It's open, and the boys don't use it. So I thought I'd take a dip." She bounced on her toes in the water and waved to the boys.

They didn't wave back.

Virgil lowered his voice. "Kathleen," he said. "Are you pregnant?"

His wife closed her eyes. She spat again, tugging a strap of her swimsuit.

How many years had it been since he'd seen that thing, he wondered. Eight years at *least*. Not since the '40s. The suit was old-fashioned, with some kind of skirt at the bottom, and Virgil didn't like the way the thin straps now cut into Kathleen's fleshy shoulders, striping her skin with red marks, hugging bone. The material was so worn it thinned around her breasts, and Virgil realized with horror that if he looked closely, he could see his wife's nipples, round as bullseyes.

The whole apparatus looked like it could fall apart at any second.

Virgil moved himself into a squatting position at the edge of the pool, like his old swim coach from college. Unlike his wife, he was no athlete; he'd only swum for one semester, and never won a meet. Losing never bothered him. Though on the short side, Virgil Beckett had been one of the most attractive men on campus—people called him "Coop," after Gary Cooper— so he wasn't competitive. When he was a boy, his mother, a willowy blond stunner named Elizabeth—Bitsy—had told him not to worry: good-looking people didn't have to be.

Virgil tried not to think about his neighbors who had appeared, standing on their balconies. They were elderly, with nothing better to do after church, before lunch.

A few were pointing.

The scene was beginning to remind him of a time back in

Pawtucket before the boys were born, when Kathy surprised him at work wearing a trench coat with nothing but her nightgown on beneath it. The nightgown, long and wrinkled, had shown beneath the bottom of the trench coat. It made her look nuts. He would have preferred it if she were naked, he'd always thought, and now here she was in the swimming pool, in November.

"Stop *bouncing* like that, for God's sake," he said.

Kathleen stared at the water. "Why?"

Virgil cringed. He wasn't rigid, nor was he in his best form if something fell out of order. For his entire life, he had preferred to follow through with whatever arrangements had been constructed for him.

He had been to the war, like everyone else, and for most men, the experience had either energized them into leadership or destroyed them. It had done neither to Virgil Beckett. In May of '44 he was shipped off to Italy for an attack on southern France that never materialized, and spent two weeks sightseeing around the ruins of Naples in a daze. When he twisted his ankle taking out some trash, he faked that it was broken, and ended up crutching around the hospital for two weeks more, flirting with the Italian nurses until they agreed to send him home. That fall, when he enrolled at the University of Delaware, he kept up the limping for a while because the girls all seemed to like him wounded. It was how he met Kathleen.

One wet October day on campus, Virgil was killing the afternoon in the library's audio booth with his ankle up, resting his arms on his crutches. He was listening to Charlie Parker records, fantasizing about being a member of a famous jazz quartet, playing the saxophone in a huge theater, in front of a crowd. He liked "Hot House" and "Anthropology" best, but also the slower ones, like "All the Things You Are." It's what he was listening to when he noticed a slender brunette sitting at a table outside his booth, reading. Her brown hair, thick and shiny, was divided in half, and she wore a white dress with a fulsome, pleated skirt.

Virgil stared at the dress for many minutes before realizing it was a tennis outfit.

When he got up the courage to leave, he hobbled past the table and felt a charge in his body when she looked up at him, whispered, "*Faker*," and smiled.

Though no Bitsy Beckett, Kathleen Lovelace was pretty and worked her best features with makeup. She laughed easily, which made her pretty. The first time they did more than kiss, he snuck in through the window of her room at Warner Hall, and she apparently knew what was going to happen before he did: her roommate would be gone for two hours, she said. She had changed the sheets.

Virgil didn't know what he'd expected but was pleasantly surprised when Kathleen sat him down on her bed and declared that, for obvious reasons, there could be no penetration, and offered him a short list of acceptable substitutes. He had forgotten to bring a condom anyway, he told her sheepishly. Kathy knew what she liked and when she liked it. She had no desire to try anything new, and this wouldn't change, not in three years of dating nor nine years of marriage. She didn't tell him about other boys; he never asked. He welcomed her to snuggle into his armpit (she called it Muskrat Dungeon), relieved that he had met this tall girl happy to be in charge of everything. Virgil Beckett felt easy and comfortable around Kathleen Lovelace, so when they were both seniors, he offered her a ring, which she accepted. Though he had worried occasionally about Kathy over the years, Virgil had never, not once, worried that the marriage itself wouldn't work.

"So are you coming inside?"

Kathleen shook her head.

Virgil put a hand in the pool water. "People get the flu for less, you know," he said.

"I don't think so," his wife said, peeling a few wet strands of hair from her neck. "I feel wonderful, actually. But if you're cold, you should go inside." She swung her head and smiled. "I'm just having a dip, that's all," she said. "Tell the boys they can join me if they want."

Virgil looked up at his balcony, where his sons remained standing in their little church suits. Their arms were crossed. "I'll bring you a towel," he said.

"I have a towel," Kathleen said.

A folded blue towel was on the grass, next to the pool cover.

The cover was a massive beige thing, which, when removed from its position over the swimming pool, resembled a collapsed tent. Virgil wondered how on earth Kathleen had moved it by herself. It occurred to him that someone must have helped her.

Cosmo, he thought.

Kosmas Parousia Jr., a Delaware Greek, was the landlord

and general operations manager of Acropolis Place Apartments. A short, black-haired, smooth-cheeked man who doused himself daily with what Virgil estimated to be great lashings of Pinaud Clubman aftershave, Cosmo had a shocking, high-pitched laugh often heard echoing throughout the complex. He had taken over management of the place two years ago, after his father died, and wore shorts almost year-round. Occasionally, Virgil spotted Cosmo's stumped, hairy legs sticking out from underneath the chassis of a person's car.

Privately, Kathleen called him "The Little Troll," but Virgil liked him. Cosmo and his wife had two boys just a year older than Nicholas and Nathaniel. The Beckett and Parousia boys didn't get along but on nice afternoons tolerated one another, helpless to the urge to be out of doors. Cosmo was a good manager, alert to the needs of his tenants, and this morning, Virgil briefly feared that their landlord had seen Kathleen in that ancient, see-through bathing suit.

"Well, all right, then," he said, and gave Kathleen a kiss on the top of her head. He left the pool and climbed the stairs for a second time, calling out to the balcony: "Mother says you can join her swimming, if you want," and made for the linen closet, where his wife kept the firm stack of towels, the tidy arrangement of balms and lotions. Coppertone for the boys.

Whether here in Newark or back in Pawtucket, Kathleen kept their home immaculate, which Virgil appreciated. She was not someone who could sit still for very long. Most of the novels she owned had been dog-eared.

Virgil grabbed two towels from the top of the pile, returned to the balcony, and gave them to the boys, who were still standing, staring at their mother.

"Go inside," he said. "Go get changed, then you can go in the pool."

"We're not swimming," Nicholas said.

"Your mother's swimming," he said. "You boys should go swimming too."

"*Why* is she swimming," said Nicholas.

"It's *November*," said Nathaniel.

"Because it's nice out. It doesn't matter," said Virgil. "You two go outside. I'm playing golf. If you don't want to swim, then go to the park."

"We're *already* outside, and we don't *want* to go to the park," Nicholas said.

Nathaniel, the eldest, was tall and quiet with dark brown hair like his mother. A joyful, chatty fellow when he was little, recently the boy had retreated into himself somewhat, allowing Nicholas to manage things. Still, Virgil knew he heard and considered everything. Nathaniel was a good student, and seemed happiest when allowed to watch television.

Nicholas, on the other hand, was Bitsy Beckett all over again. His blond hair was so light it looked white. He was handsome but small, and defensive about being small. Teachers didn't like him, and reports from school almost always contained, in delicate cursive, "recalcitrant." The word was repeated so often, Virgil speculated that the teachers told one another what to write, from year to year. The other word they used was "prevaricator." Nicholas lied regularly, and without remorse. Virgil and Kathleen thought he just liked telling stories, like his grandfather, and tried explaining that to his teachers, but it was clear that the verdict on Nicholas had been cast early, and Virgil knew his youngest son would likely suffer until he left school altogether. Nicholas was also sensitive, prone to colds, headaches, and other minor physical grievances, which made him even more pitiful. Sometimes, when Virgil looked at his two sons, he wondered if things had not been unfairly distributed in their mother's womb.

This morning, Virgil glared at his youngest. "Well, what do you want to do?"

"We want to watch Mother swim," Nicholas said.

"Fine," he said. "Do whatever you want."

The phone rang.

Virgil left the balcony and went inside. He picked up the receiver. If Kathy would just leave the pool, he thought, then he could relax and have a proper day off. He was already starting to feel the afternoon slipping away from him. There was no question that this would be the last day of the season, and although he typically disliked people who exaggerated, he knew that to miss out on the game today really would color the whole week.

"Beckett," a voice said. "It's Wooz. We're hitting the links in thirty minutes. You in? The sun won't last."

"I'll be there," Virgil said, and hung up.

He crossed the living room and looked through the sliding glass door, where the boys had already established themselves on the edge of the balcony, watching their mother lean against the far side of the swimming pool, stretching her neck. They had changed into their summer play clothes, and their bare legs dangled between the iron bars. They had also helped themselves to two cherry Popsicles.

"You boys should eat something," he said. "I'll make tuna fish, then your father is going golfing."

Virgil wandered into the kitchen. He glanced at the cabinet where Kathleen stored her vast assortment of baking flours, powders, oils, and gelatins. He really tried not to drink much anymore, but kept a little whiskey for himself for such occasions, hidden behind a large tub of White Colonel lard. This morning he opened the cabinet, grabbed the bottle, and poured himself a short one.

Except for the occasional Aperol spritz, Kathleen was uninterested in alcohol, and Virgil did not like to drink in front of her. Back in Pawtucket, he used to stop at Crooly's Bar on the way home before dinner. If he felt like tying one on, he stayed at Crooly's longer. He didn't do that kind of thing anymore. More than a few times, Virgil had gone and drunk too much, and gotten himself into something he shouldn't have. He always woke up feeling a little guilty. It passed.

Virgil didn't love any of the girls, but there had been one he'd fallen harder for than he knew was safe. Her real name was Imogene Monson, but at Crooly's she went by the nickname "Little Mo." She was a cocktail waitress, a tiny redhead with Tinker Bell legs. The men at the bar harassed Little Mo constantly, talking openly about the color of her pubic hair, which shocked Virgil until he understood it was a game: they faked actually caring about it, and she faked being mad at them. They always tipped her well.

Virgil thought Little Mo could be some kind of model if anyone ever discovered her in that lousy bar in Pawtucket, and one night last April, after months of flirting, he told her so before they slept together on the old leather couch in the back room of Crooly's.

As he stared down at Imogene Monson's tight, milky waist, Virgil Beckett had not anticipated how much he would enjoy watching the famous, fire-colored pubis go to work on him. She massaged his shoulders with her small hands and whispered in his ear the whole time, calling him "Charlie" because he always played "Confirmation," the Charlie Parker bebop number, on the juke.

The next morning, he'd woken up next to Kathleen with a headache, thinking hotly about Little Mo. During lunch at work, he found a note she had slipped into his coat pocket, *don't forget about me Charlie xoxo—M.O.*, and Virgil liked how she'd signed the note wrong, like her nickname was initials. By the end of the day, though, when the girl was still on his mind, Virgil knew he had to—as his father would say—"nip the situation in the bud." After work, he went straight to Crooly's, brought Little Mo by the elbow to the back room, and sat her down on the couch. He put his arm around her while he explained that he was sorry, but he couldn't see her again. He held her hands while she cried. Afterward, he promised himself on the drive home that from here on out, things would be different. He would quit Crooly's, and make more of a commitment to Kathleen.

It was easier than he would have guessed. Whether his wife noticed that he'd cleaned up his act or not, she never said, but she seemed happy. The boys seemed happy. Six months ago, he quit his job and they sold their house and left Pawtucket. They returned to Newark, Delaware, where they both had gone to college.

It was Virgil's idea to bring the family to church each week. It's what people did. He ate dinner at home every night now, the four of them at the little table in the kitchen, as there was no proper dining room in the apartment at Acropolis Place.

2.

Eight weeks, Kathleen Beckett guessed. She was about eight weeks along, and based on what she knew of her first two pregnancies, everything was going just as it should.

It was Sunday. November. Warm for this time of year.

Kathleen remained in bed until she heard Virgil ushering the boys outside, into the Bluebird, then rose slowly, waited for the ache of nausea to warm her body, and ran to the bathroom to throw up.

They had been married for nine years and dated through college, but it wasn't until six months ago, when they moved back to Delaware, that Virgil said he wanted to start going to church. One night last April, her husband had come home from work as usual, taken a long shower, and when he emerged, wiping his head with a towel, he said he wouldn't be missing dinner anymore. And he thought they should start going to church.

Not one week later, he quit his job. All he told Kathleen was that it was time for a change. And they might have to leave Pawtucket. And how did she feel about that.

Kathleen, for her part, was thrilled. She wouldn't mind leaving Rhode Island *one bit*, she said. They had been living in the yellow house on South Bend Street for almost ten years, ever since '48, but the boys were bigger now. She could understand Virgil wanting to move, and was happy about it, but found his sudden desire to go to church frankly — bizarre. Up till then, all her husband had ever wanted to do was go golfing or lie around the house, listening to bebop or jazz. Charlie Parker in particular, though he also liked others with names Kathleen could never remember: Sonny Rollins, Thelonious Monk, Dizzy Gillespie, Stan Getz. Kathleen always knew when Virgil was home from work: one of his records would start spinning the moment he walked in the door.

Her husband was a good-looking, good-natured guy from Monterey, California. He once saw Charlie Parker perform in Monterey, and there had been some talk a while back about his wanting to play the saxophone, but as of yet no follow-through, so it was the definitiveness of the church announcement more than anything that surprised Kathleen.

They started attending the first Sunday they arrived back in Newark.

They had settled on the First Presbyterian in Wilmington, even though it was a drive to get there. Virgil liked it because it was huge, a big stone Gothic revival with a narrowly pitched gable roof, stained-glass lancet windows, and granite buttresses that reminded him of a cathedral he once saw in Italy. Kathleen didn't feel one way or the other about it: it was the church she'd attended as a girl. The building was beautiful, Kathleen agreed, but in that old-fashioned, severe sort of way. The pews were still lined with red velvet. White wooden paneling with gilded trim rose up to a garish gold pulpit from which the Reverend Andrew Underhill spoke.

Kathleen didn't know him. "Reverend Andy," as he introduced himself to the ladies, was young and raffishly plump — much too fat for someone so young, Kathleen thought — and had a voice so soft it sounded stolen. He had replaced Reverend Wallis a few years back, whom Kathleen and her parents had known and liked. Reverend Andrew Underhill was partial to Ephesians, and read from it so often, Kathleen wondered if there wasn't something wrong with him:

"Walk in the way of love," he said quietly each Sunday, *"just as Christ loved us and gave himself up for us as a fragrant offering and sacrifice to God."*

Whenever Kathleen shook his hands, she could see that he filed and buffed his fingernails. They had only been attending his services for six months, but the young man had called upon

Kathleen more than a few times now, hoping to be invited to dinner.

I would be a reverend, she often thought, *if there was someone to make me dinner every night.*

This morning Kathleen left the bathroom and started to clean up. It didn't take long. Their apartment, 14B, was smaller than the house in Pawtucket, and temporary. Most of their belongings were still in boxes downstairs, locked in the Acropolis Place storage room. Virgil initially said they would rent the apartment just for a month, just while they looked for a house close to his new job in Wilmington, but one month quickly stretched into three. Then six. "Definitely by November," he'd said, and now Virgil was thinking Christmas. Maybe after.

Kathleen made the beds. She balled up the clothes the boys had left on the floor of the room they now shared, and made her way into the kitchen. When she discovered that Virgil had left scrambled eggs in the pan, she uncontrollably retched, twice, into the kitchen sink. Afterward, resting her chin on her wrist to catch her breath, she turned on the faucet, full blast. She washed everything. Then she remembered that Virgil kept a bottle of something behind the White Colonel lard in the cabinet. She moved the tub with the Revolutionary soldier on it aside, and there it was.

Kathleen unscrewed the cap and sipped the whiskey straight, which helped. From her experiences with Nicholas and Nathaniel, she knew that a tiny bit of alcohol was fine, particularly on days she felt queer.

The phone rang.

Kathleen steadied herself for a moment, then answered it. When she learned who it was on the line, she blew all the air out her nose.

"Good morning, Mr. Beckett. How are you?" she said, and glanced at the clock in the kitchen. It was six thirty in the morning out there. To Coke Beckett, it was six thirty in the morning all over the world.

"I'm looking for my son," Virgil's father said.

When Kathleen met Colson Beckett on the day of her wedding, it was instantly clear who her new husband got his looks from. Coke's face looked like an old baseball glove. Kathleen couldn't tell the difference between wrinkles and scars. His hair, which he miraculously hadn't lost, stood upright on his head in a shock of white, and he sported a matching wiry white beard that Virgil said he never trimmed, and that never grew longer. When Virgil informed her that his father was just fifty-two, Kathleen was stunned. His teeth were the color of mustard, and his voice crackled with phlegm. The man was always smoking. That summer, when she and Virgil went to see *The Treasure of the Sierra Madre*, they were in hysterics that Coke was exactly like the old gold digger.

This past July, just after they'd settled into the new apartment, Coke had called to say he wasn't feeling well — something in the chest, Virgil said, and complaining was unlike him. Irenie, Virgil's youngest sister, had finally married some kind of machinist from Oregon, and Virgil was worried about Coke being on his own, so in early August, after having just packed and moved from Rhode Island to Delaware, the whole family took the cross-country trip to see him.

They drove for two long, hot weeks with the boys in their new Buick Bluebird to Big Sur, California, and stayed in the shingled, one-bedroom cabin in the mountains where Coke now lived.

When they arrived, Kathleen found Virgil's now sixty-one-year-old father in fine fettle. He just wanted company. For hours, even though the sun was shining and it was a perfectly unbeatable day, and neither Kathleen nor the boys had ever been to California, Coke kept them all inside the cabin's smoky little sitting area, telling them stories about what had happened in the Great War (at least he made sure to save the most gruesome tales for when the boys were asleep, Kathleen thought). When not talking about the war, Coke was either riding Kathleen for trying to tidy up the place or talking about his movie experience in Hollywood—how he once was drinking a Pabst at a bar and was selected, on the spot, by a director to act in a movie called *The Dubious Few*, which neither Kathleen nor Virgil had ever seen.

He played a cowboy, he said, who sat on top of a horse and wore a ten-gallon hat. His job was to scowl at the main character, and he had one line that changed every time Coke told it: *"Sounds like trouble, Mr. Jephson!"* or *"Lookout, Mr. Jephson!"* or *"Somebody's got it in for you, Jephson!"* or *"Oneathem bullets got yer name on it, Jephson!"*

Coke Beckett talked about the numerous fish he'd caught, "steelhead fresh from the Big Sur River," or huge saltwater rockfish and lingcod "right here, down at the beach." In a rusted Danker's Coffee tin on the shelf above a makeshift metal tub that worked as a kitchen sink, next to a pot of withering marigolds, Coke kept a stash of natural jade he said he'd collected from the caves of Big Sur, by the spray.

He told the boys it was the fortune they would inherit when he died.

Kathleen and Virgil had planned to stay for three weeks, but the boys had to camp outside, and Coke smoked from the moment he got up in the morning until bedtime. In the end, they lasted only nine days before packing up the Bluebird and making the long eastward drive home.

"He and the boys are at church, Mr. Beckett," Kathleen said. "Can I help you? How are you?"

There was a shuffling of papers on the other end of the line, and Kathleen heard him strike a match.

"No, you can't," he said. "I've got some business for Virgil. You tell him to call me as soon as he can."

"I will. It's so nice to hear from you, Coke," Kathleen said.

He hung up.

Kathleen knew that Colson Beckett never said goodbye on the phone. Calls from California were too expensive for goodbyes, and Virgil had long ago instructed Kathleen not to be offended. More than once, Virgil had been midsentence when his father decided he'd spent enough, and just hung up on him.

Kathleen returned the receiver to its cradle. She dried and put away the dishes, wiped down the sink and counters, and took the opportunity to wet and polish the kitchen window.

Then she left the apartment and went downstairs to the laundry room, returning with the clothes she'd left in the Acropolis Place communal dryer overnight. While she folded, she lit a cigarette and turned on the small portable transistor radio she kept in the kitchen. She listened to half of an Elvis song.

On Friday, she and Virgil had plans to drive into Wilmington to see *Jailhouse Rock* at the Queen Theater. Kathleen didn't like Elvis, she thought his face looked like a cheese danish, but the movie was starring Judy Tyler, who they saw over the summer in *Bop Girl Goes Calypso*. It was a silly picture, but Virgil liked it, and afterward, walking back to the car, he had whispered in her ear that she looked just like Judy Tyler, and kissed her cheek.

The next day, she read in *Ladies' Home Journal* that Judy Tyler had been killed in a car wreck in Wyoming.

Kathleen's own parents had died years ago, from two different kinds of cancer. Her father, Walter Lovelace, had been a lieutenant commander in the Navy. He'd liked baseball, and boxed some. He collected miniature train sets, and every Christmas sent one running a wide circle around the base of the tree. The passenger cars were filled with tiny businessmen carrying tiny presents on their laps. The locomotive, which Kathleen was not allowed to touch, had a working headlamp and used smoke fluid for steam.

Ruth, Kathleen's mother, loved dancing. She was from Philadelphia, where her father held a faculty appointment at the Wharton School of Finance and Commerce. They were introduced at a reception for an ROTC affair at UPenn, where

Walter was receiving a naval commendation and about to join the faculty himself. Ignoring the decade between them, and at the urging of their parents, they married, and in 1920, Ruth moved with Walter into his family house, a two-story mansard in the Highlands of Wilmington, Delaware. Before Kathleen was born, Ruth taught after-school dance classes at the local elementary. She taught Kathleen how to waltz in their kitchen.

Ruth and Walter Lovelace were generous with money if not affection. Kathleen had no brothers or sisters. Whenever she bugged her mother about it, Ruth would snap at her to *stop asking.* Her father had simply wanted to see what kind of child she would be before deciding on a sibling, her mother said, and from an early age, Kathleen had displayed an affable, obeisant demeanor, so her parents had stopped at one. If she had been difficult, Ruth told her, they would have had another to ease the blow, and as a result, Kathleen was often alone as a child, though never certain she was suited to be. The house was much too big for three people. Kathleen would wander from room to room, looking for something she had never seen before. She occasionally played with the neighborhood children who remained in Wilmington during the summers, who were always welcomed into the house by Ruth, but Kathleen was tall, and stood out for being tall. For the most part, other girls either tormented or bored her, so much of her time was spent in a small alcove in the living room, lying stomach-down on the carpet doing homework, reading, or drawing.

Kathleen most ardently wished she had a sibling when Ruth and Walter argued. Her parents' fights were frequent and loud.

She knew they loved each other in their way, and Kathleen neither held it against them nor believed they fought more than anybody else's parents. One night, though, the yelling was so awful that she opened her bedroom window, hoisted herself onto the roof, and stayed there for the hours it took for her parents to notice her missing. She made the decision that if she ever got married—and she doubted she would—it would only be to someone who hated conflict as much as she did.

So it went until Kathleen turned sixteen, and everything suddenly changed.

She attended Tower Hill, the nearby private school, and while walking home one afternoon, Kathleen passed a group of four women wearing white skirts. Tennis racquets rested on their shoulders like rifles. Kathleen asked the women who they were, and they replied that they were students at the Women's College of Delaware. A college team.

Kathleen announced to her parents over dinner that she wanted to play tennis. And she was going to attend the Women's College of Delaware. The following week, when she returned home from school, she went into her bedroom and on her bed was a gift from her father: a brand-new wooden Dunlop Gold Wing with a robin's-egg-blue throat, a pair of gold wings beneath the bridge, and a long black rubber handle. Ruth and Walter Lovelace didn't see much of their daughter after that.

She was always at the courts.

The summer before Kathleen's junior year of high school, an advertisement for tennis lessons appeared on the Tower Hill community bulletin board, underscored by a local phone number. In a gesture of what Kathleen viewed as uncharacteristic hospitality, her parents contacted and hired a foreign student, Billy Blasko, to teach Kathleen Lovelace the game of tennis.

His real name, she would learn, was Viliam Blaško, and he was from a Jewish family in southern Czechoslovakia, a small border town right on the Danube remarkable only for being home to a bridge that had been bombed in the First World War and then rebuilt. When other families heard what the Lovelaces had done, they signed up their daughters. People said it was a way to help the young man and his family, and so it was that as July of 1942 began, Billy Blasko had arranged for himself a tidy income to support his studies of English and biology, and the company of a group of teenage girls who all arrived on the court bearing massive crushes on the Czechoslovakian tennis ambassador. He was twenty-one.

The first day, Billy distributed a handful of cheap metal batons to practice with, the kind the girls twirled in Fourth of July parades.

"What are these for?" Kathleen asked.

Billy shrugged, and did not smile. (Kathleen would learn he never smiled.)

"First, you hit with stick," he said. "Then racquet."

Kathleen tucked her Dunlop Gold Wing under her armpit and lit a cigarette. She corrected him. "*The* stick," she said. "*The* racquet."

She didn't know what the other girls were fooling themselves about. A fully grown adult by anyone's standards, Billy

Blasko was a head taller than Kathleen with round brown eyes set deep in their sockets, and augmented by the longest eyelashes she'd ever seen on a man. His eyebrows, thick and angular, looked like bent caterpillars. Curly brown hair flopped over his forehead, and he wore snug white cotton shorts with the waist set as high as a woman's.

While the other girls twirled their batons, flirting with Billy, he told them over and over, *"Dobry,"* which meant "good." Everything was *doh-bree* with Billy and the girls, but Kathleen was serious about wanting to learn tennis and by the end of the first week considered quitting.

As it turned out, she didn't have to. Two girls got tired of the batons and quit. The other two decided to go to swimming camp after all. It was Billy and Kathleen.

As soon as they were alone together, Billy's English improved. He told her he was glad it was the two of them because he knew from the moment he saw her Dunlop Gold Wing that she was serious, and not like the others. His father, he said, was Petr Blaško, the famous Czech tennis champion who had competed in the '08 Olympics in London, and Billy didn't like wasting his father's lessons on unserious people. He didn't even need the money that badly. His parents had wisely sent most of their money with him to the United States in '37, but now his whole family, he told Kathleen, was stuck in Europe. He could not say, for certain, where they were. He said he couldn't think about it or it would make him sick. He just wanted to play tennis.

When he told her this, Kathleen softened toward Billy, and

every afternoon for the month of July, they met at the Tower Hill tennis courts behind the field house of her high school.

To start, Billy said, Kathleen had to learn the geography of the game. She needed to understand "the rectangle," he said, and spoke a crazy, unpronounceable word: the "*obdĺžnik,*" he said. Every day before the lesson, they walked the length of the court together, and Kathleen was impressed when Billy walked baseline to baseline with his eyes closed. He told her she couldn't be a real player until she could do the same thing. Kathleen closed her eyes and walked, counting her steps, and after a few days discovered that she could do it without counting at all. She memorized the placement of the net, the service line, left and right service courts, the alley line, until she could find them all blind. "Everyone thinks tennis is about hitting," Billy said. "It is actually about *póza.* Posture. How to stand, how to move. You have to know where you are at all times."

Kathleen had to learn how to step, walk, and run all over again, and Billy showed her footwork patterns that reminded her of her mother's foxtrot.

Tennis, Billy agreed, was exactly like a kind of dance.

When it was finally time to learn how to hit, Billy showed her the serve, the approach. The volley, half volley. There was the forehand, the backhand, the flat and side spin, the chip, chop, carve, the block and slice, the topspin and Kathleen's favorite, the smash. At the end of the month, when Billy said she was *dobrý,* she knew he meant it.

As Kathleen recalled the afternoon now, folding laundry in the living room of 14B, listening to Elvis croon, the smell of hot, baked earth rose up from beneath the newly laid clay. From two courts over came the yelps of basketball players, dropping their balls. A car drove by, once or twice, but that was all she remembered before Billy whispered, *"Katarina,"* and slid his fingers down her arm until they were holding hands. He led her behind the high school to the middle of an overgrown field where girls practiced field hockey in autumn, and there they met every afternoon until the end of summer, when Billy returned for his senior year at UD and Kathleen entered the eleventh grade.

Two years later, when Kathleen herself was enrolled at UD and met Virgil Beckett, she didn't have a reason *not* to tell him about Billy Blasko; nor did she have any particular reason to. Virgil never asked.

Kathleen finished folding the boys' clothes, and the phone rang again. She jumped up to answer it.

"Beckett residence," she said.

"Hiya," a woman said.

"May I ask who's calling?" Kathleen said.

"I don't know," the woman said, and hiccupped. *"May* you?"

Kathleen cinched the receiver with her shoulder and rested her back against the wall.

Last April, just before Virgil announced that he wouldn't be missing dinner anymore, he arrived home one night very late. It was a Wednesday, she recalled. Virgil being drunk on a Wednesday wasn't uncommon—her husband usually went out drinking Wednesdays and Thursdays to get himself through the week—but this time he returned in uniquely bad shape. Kathleen couldn't believe he'd driven himself home, but there he was, half asleep against the front door, his clothes and hair all messed up. He slid along a wall in the living room and gave her a terrible smile. Kathleen was glad the boys were asleep. "Virgil," she said. "My God, look at you. Are you all right?"

Virgil rolled his eyes and sneered at her. *"Are you all right,"* he said.

Her husband had never gotten angry at her before, not really, and never while drinking. Wine and beer usually made Virgil Beckett sweet and tired. She put him to bed, and the next morning, when she told him what he'd said to her, there was no memory of it. "Oh, Kath," he said, laughing. "God, I'm sorry. I really shouldn't have drunk that much."

As soon as Kathleen heard the woman's voice on the phone, she thought of Virgil, sliding along that wall.

"Who is this," she said.

"Did Charlie get it?" the woman said.

"Pardon?" Kathleen said. "Who?"

"Ask him! Did he *get* it?"

"I think you have the wrong number," Kathleen said.

The woman hung up.

Kathleen placed the receiver on the cradle and looked through the sliding glass door to where the morning sun glowed ochre on the white balcony. She followed it.

The Acropolis Place apartment complex was shaped like a pentagon. Each angle of the building took on an equal composition of light and shadow, Kathleen realized. She looked down at the blue water shining beneath her. Someone had removed the cover from the community swimming pool. A narrow concrete path surrounded it, and the rest of the courtyard was covered in dry grass. The flat surface of the water glistened.

Cosmo, she thought, and their stump-legged, hirsute Greek landlord appeared in her mind just as Kathleen Beckett realized she was covered in sweat.

5.

Virgil quickly washed out the whiskey glass and returned the bottle to its place behind the White Colonel, then packed a bag for the afternoon: his two-tone wingtip golf shoes, a change of pants and shirt. The pair of black silk socks that Kathleen had bought him for his last birthday. He ducked into the bathroom for his deodorant and grabbed his comb. Into his thirties now, Virgil was pleased that his hair was still full and bright blond. He admired the look of it as he groomed himself with the old-fashioned folding comb that had belonged to his father. It was made out of real buffalo horn.

When people told Virgil they thought Coke Beckett was a cold man, which had happened quite a bit when he was young, he shrugged them off: Bitsy's husband was one of the only men in Monterey who'd kept a steady income throughout the Depression. Coke had worked building schools and laying macadam. He taught a survival course at the Presidio for field artillery units called Atypical Emergency In-Field Medical Techniques, and even assisted the doctor in Monterey when he could. He had a story about a Japanese abalone diver who was forced to cut off his own finger when it got stuck in the shoals underwater. Coke sewed it back on. Virgil's father was a World War I veteran, and had shelled bridges and roads in the Battle of Château-Thierry and the Battle of Soissons. He'd played a cowboy in a real Hollywood picture, *The Dubious Few*, and, with little to go around, raised Virgil and his three sisters with Bitsy right up until she walked in front of a bus.

What more did you want out of a man?

Virgil was proud of his father, but it wouldn't be until Virgil came back from Naples that Coke was proud of him. "How many?" his father asked, and Virgil told him that he had killed two, two Nazis, and his father was content with the answer. Virgil had considered saying three or four, but knew that Coke wouldn't believe he could handle any more than two, and would be disappointed if he said only one. This way, Virgil never worried about telling the lie, and Coke had never questioned his telling it.

His father had no way of knowing that he never made it to France, and Naples had already been liberated for eight months by the time Virgil arrived. The only violence he witnessed came from the Neapolitans expressing their grief and their poverty. In March, two months before he got there, Vesuvius had erupted, blanketing a foot of ash over buildings that were already in ruins.

Virgil tossed the comb into his bag and went to the living room closet, where he kept his clubs. The golf bag, made of leather and metal, weighed twenty-five pounds. He hoisted it over one shoulder, the bag of clothes over the other, and left 14B. He went downstairs once more, and over to the pool, where Kathleen appeared to be watching her painted toenails bob in the water.

"I'm going golfing," he said.

"Sounds good," said his wife.

Virgil noticed that Kathleen had set up her University of Delaware ashtray and their portable radio at the edge of the pool. Behind her was the staccato thrum of a newscaster.

"What's going on," he said.

"The Russians sent up another one," she said.

"What other one?"

"*Sputnik 2*," said Kathleen.

Mr. and Mrs. Beckett looked up at the sky.

There were no clouds. Was it only a month ago that the occupants of Acropolis Place had all stood on their balconies looking up at the stars, some through binoculars, trying to see the first Russian satellite crawling across the heavens? In the weeks that followed, Virgil made sure the boys didn't listen to the news, though he couldn't say for sure what they heard at school. He didn't know how Kathy felt about it, but he personally thought the whole world was making a big deal out of nothing, and imagined she felt the same way. Eisenhower himself had dismissed it. *"They have put one small ball in the air,"* the president said on the radio. There was no threat to the United States.

"They sent a dog up this time," Kathleen said.

Virgil looked at her. "A dog?"

"People are calling her 'Muttnik.' I think it's terrible. Who could do that? Send a darling little dog up there to die."

Virgil did not know what to say.

"The dog won't die," he said finally. "People plan for this sort of thing. I'm sure they planned it. I certainly wouldn't worry about it, if that's what's bothering you."

Kathleen shoved her body off the wall and sailed away from him, into the center of the pool.

"Kathy," he said.

His wife play-splashed him and smiled. "I'm fine. I feel much better now that I'm in the pool. It's cooler here. The heat's awful, don't you think?"

She took a deep breath and sank beneath the surface.

"Is everything all right?" a voice shouted.

Mrs. Donovan, the elderly lady who lived alone up in 3C, had appeared like a little ghost on her balcony. Virgil and Kathleen brought Mrs. Donovan her supper on Sundays. They had never done anything like that before in Pawtucket, helping their neighbors, but at Reverend Andy's urging, now they helped Mrs. Donovan. Most of the occupants of

Acropolis Place, they discovered when they moved in, were old people.

"We're fine, Mrs. Donovan," Virgil shouted. "Everything's fine. Everything's good here. Kathy's having a swim, that's all. You can go back inside."

Two more white-haired neighbors floated onto their balconies. Virgil didn't know them.

"She'll catch her death!" one shouted.

Virgil suddenly felt like he was in a movie.

"Don't worry about it," he shouted back. "She's just having a dunk. It's hot out today, isn't it? It's got to be seventy. Maybe eighty."

"But it's *November*," Mrs. Donovan said. "The air's not right."

Kathleen was still underwater.

The men at Equitable had spoken of "episodes" with their wives, and Virgil worried that's what this was turning into. A bona fide episode. Whatever it was, Kathleen's reason for being in the pool wasn't anyone's business but his own, he thought, and waved Mrs. Donovan back into her apartment until, reluctantly, she retreated.

But Virgil saw how she kept watching them from behind her curtains.

Next to his feet, dried red and orange leaves blew into the pool, scattering the light. His wife appeared to be sitting at the bottom of the pool with her knees hugged tightly to her chest. Her body, round and moving, abruptly jerked, and then, in a gasp, Kathleen breached the surface.

"Is that it?" Virgil said. "Are you all cooled off and everything?"

"I'm going to stay in a while longer," she said.

Virgil unconsciously tugged at his shirtsleeves. From somewhere close by, another flock of Canada geese sounded their bicycle horns.

"Look, Kath, I have to go. Who's going to watch the boys?"

Kathleen looked up at their two sons perched on the balcony of 14B. "I'm watching them, and they look fine," she said. "We're all fine."

Virgil stood up straight, adjusting the strap of his golf bag. It wasn't that he didn't trust Kathleen—nothing had ever gone so wrong that there was a reason not to *trust* her—but there was the one time at the house in Pawtucket, a few months after Nathaniel was born, that he'd come home to find her soaking in the bathtub while the baby was in the next room, screaming. "Jesus, Kathleen," he'd yelled. "Don't you hear him? What are you doing in here?"

His wife didn't answer. She lifted one leg out of the water, turned off the knob with a soapy foot, and looked at him innocently. "What?" she said.

Virgil reached into the tub and unplugged it. The bathwater was freezing.

That time he actually called California and asked Coke about it, but his father didn't seem to think there was anything odd.

Coke Beckett had taken cold showers every morning of his life.

"Okay, well, I'm off, then," Virgil said, and jangled his keys out from his pocket. He went to the carport, opened the trunk of the Bluebird, and shoved his golf bag inside. He walked around to the driver's side door and got in. Even though the carport gave shade, it was still unbearably hot. The seats were new vinyl and smelled like they could melt. The back of Virgil's thighs burned when he sat, and he quickly rolled down the window, touching his hands to the wheel a few times before they got used to the temperature. He inserted the key into the ignition. He would play nine holes instead of eighteen, he thought, that was all. People were probably going to want to listen to the news anyway. Virgil backed the car out of the carport and shouted from the window: "I'll be back in a few hours!"

No one answered him.

He turned on the radio and drove away from Acropolis Place, taking the right-hand turn toward Louviers Country Club, one hundred and forty acres of smooth green grass located not six miles away.

4.

Kathleen knew virtually nothing about California, where her husband grew up. In August, when she saw the cabin where Virgil's father lived—little more than a big shack with a telephone, really, wedged into the Santa Lucia Mountains above the ocean in a way that seemed uniquely precarious— and while she sat there listening to all of Coke's stories about murdering people, about fingers being cut off and sewn on, about being cast in movies or catching all those stupid fish, she wondered not for the first time why she had agreed to marry Virgil Beckett.

It was the spring of 1948, right after her final intercollegiate tennis championship. Kathleen would graduate in a month, and she had just beaten Linda Kent, the top-ranked player from the University of Maryland, in sixteen games, on the match point. When Kathleen won, the crowd had given her a standing ovation. Dr. William Carlson, president of the University of Delaware, there with his daughter, walked down the bleachers and waited in line to shake her hand. He told her she had *remarkable* endurance for a woman player, playing sixteen games in a row like that. The man, a Legion of Merit recipient who'd spent the war creating airbases in the arctic, said he'd never seen anything like it, and embarrassed Kathleen when he grabbed her wrist and held her hand in the air like it was his own.

Kathleen posed on the court for photos, one of which Dr. Carlson ordered to be printed and framed, and he had it hung in the Memorial Library next to other accomplished young women who had graduated.

The University of Delaware had only recently gone coed, absorbing the Women's College of Delaware out of existence and into the School of Arts and Science. The new president, fielding numerous calls of alarm from the female faculty, students, alums, wanted to let the women know they had a place there, so the picture of Kathleen in her tennis dress, the head of her Dunlop Gold Wing perched on one shoulder, was hung next to three of the best-known virgins on campus: Maureen Canterbury working out a calculus problem on a chalkboard; Joanne Lubble in a lab coat in front of myriad test tubes; Meredith

Meznick holding pruning shears in the campus greenhouse. The plaque beneath the photographs, which Kathleen always disliked, said NOTABLE WOMEN OF UD.

Of course, Virgil was there. He never missed watching Kathleen play a home game, and once even borrowed someone's beat-up '36 Plymouth and filled it with friends to make an away game in New Haven. Before a match, Kathleen would sometimes glance up from the court and spot him watching her from the bleachers, and in those moments had to remind herself that the handsome boy sitting there was hers.

That October afternoon when Virgil Beckett limped his way out of the listening booth in the library, Kathleen was surprised when he stopped at the table where she was reading. The best-looking boys never paid attention to her—she was too tall—but here was this fellow called "Coop" bent over his wooden crutch, pretending to fix something on it that wasn't broken. He looked up at her through a flip of blond hair: "Tennis in the library?" he asked.

Kathleen fell into a blush. It would be months before she told him that Walter had passed away the week before; that now her mother wasn't feeling well; that Kathleen was wearing her tennis uniform because she had run out of clean clothes and didn't have anywhere to send laundry. She pointed at the Charlie Parker record he was carrying and asked if he played the saxophone.

"Do I play the saxophone," he replied.

It was two days before Kathleen realized he hadn't answered her question.

Kathleen Lovelace was not vain. She fully understood the limitations of her beauty. She had one of those faces that looked better from an angle. Her eyes were widely set, her nose crowded her upper lip—Ruth once said to tell people her features were Dutch and Belgian—but Kathleen had to admit she liked walking into the college cafeteria on Virgil Beckett's arm. The boy was broad shouldered and gifted with muscles that she would later learn he hadn't earned. He never exercised. His blond hair was parted at the side, twisted by a comb. A piece of it was always falling into his eyes, daring anyone not to adore it.

Thoughts of Billy Blasko returned to Kathleen only rarely when she was with Virgil, though when she was alone she could recall on demand every detail of every moment that had passed between them. Those hot afternoons behind the field house, lying together in frank poses of nudity, talking tennis, or the nights Kathleen slipped out from her room and met Billy for long walks along the Brandywine, past the monkeys at the zoo, and into the black city air of downtown Wilmington. The names of the storefronts and billboards were sonorous, otherworldly—the Playhouse, the Joy Trimming Company, H. F. Robelon's Piano and Organs, LeMar's 7th Heaven of Fashion—and Kathleen recalled the exhilaration she felt when a police siren cried out one night; how the car came speeding toward them in the darkness and they both jumped, hearts racing, into a dim entryway of the grand DuPont building, coming face-to-face with an array of men's dress suits donned by the window mannequins of Mansure & Prettyman—or those nights they walked all the way to the train station so Kathleen could admire the clock tower that Billy called "Romanesque." They talked about his older sisters, Elena and Ana, about whom he worried constantly, and when Billy couldn't talk about them anymore, they discussed lighter topics like Ruth's entire wardrobe of clothes that she could no longer fit into and never wore, yet delivered to the cleaner every New Year to starch and press, or Walter's odd morning habit of gargling hydrogen peroxide. Kathleen mostly listened when Billy talked about what he called *"real* subjects": the war, politics, and books (it was on Billy's prompting that she had checked out from the library a novel called *The Nazarene,* which was so big she was almost embarrassed to carry it home). Those nights they talked about the whole world, or so it seemed to Kathleen, all so they could sit together on the wooden bench inside the station's waiting area with her head on Billy's shoulder and not say anything, waiting for the lonely eye of a coming train to appear around the bend. Kathleen felt she could summon every word of those conversations between them at will, and even later that fall, when her father had driven her, stone-faced, to the private military doctor in Philadelphia, even when Walter silently dropped her off the way that he had at the corner of Walnut and 37th, neither opening the car door nor getting out, and even when Kathleen was quietly escorted by a strange man away from her father, through the Wharton campus, across Locust Walk, and into a building with a bizarre little back office that, she was told by a nurse, served as a VA clinic, and even afterward, when she was fine again, when Walter and Ruth were shouting at each other, shouting at her, prohibiting Kathleen from ever seeing The Jew again, her recollection of those two months over the summer of '42 remained utterly unspoiled.

In the spring of '48, as Virgil was watching Kathleen destroy Linda Kent on the tennis court, Walter was dead, Ruth's pancreas would not last another season, and it had been almost six years since Kathleen had seen Billy.

When he wrote her letters, which he did often, she only occasionally wrote him back. She knew he had found a job working as a research assistant at the Alfred I. duPont Institute in pediatric orthopedics. He was still in the area.

At the end of every letter, Billy said that he wanted her to visit him, and always included his phone number. Kathleen never called. She had never asked him to come see her at school, or watch her play tennis, but sometimes a feeling would come over her as she played, that Billy was there in the stands, and Kathleen, while searching the crowd for Virgil, sometimes found herself also searching for Billy. She hoped he would never come find her. She knew that if she saw him in person, he would ask her to marry him, and she did not want him to ask. She was afraid she might say yes.

In the end, Kathleen always arrived at the same conclusion: she married Virgil Beckett because he was easy. He was two inches shorter than she was, but they fit together nicely. They were, as her friend Patricia once put it, "fruit from the same bowl."

Kathleen Lovelace believed it would not be difficult to love Virgil Beckett, and knew that she could control how she felt when she was with him. Where Billy was intellectual and serious, Virgil was relaxed. Funny. They talked all the time without ever discussing. Kathleen couldn't recall if she'd ever seen Virgil with a book. Just three years had passed since the war ended, but when they were together, he never mentioned it. Outside events seemed to pass by them strangely, as though they were watching a moving world from a stationary train. When they talked, it was about their friends, Kathleen's tennis matches, or nothing at all. They never fought. When Kathleen posed for the professional photograph that would hang in Memorial Library, Virgil was standing behind the photographer, making faces, giving him bunny ears. Afterward, he took her out to dinner at the Athena Taverna, a Greek restaurant they both liked, and when he offered her an opal engagement ring over a wet diamond of baklava, she accepted it.

This morning, looking down on the pool from the balcony, Kathleen wiped sweat off her neck with two fingers, then stepped back inside, and went to the linen closet. She reached for the top shelf. There, behind her boxes of pads and Midol, was her old red bathing suit from college.

While pregnant with Nathaniel, Kathleen's weight was almost double what it should have been. The doctors told her to stop eating so much, but she tried explaining to them, perplexed, that she wasn't eating more than usual. She just swelled up. It was like her body expected to find itself in a car crash in six months and was preparing the requisite padding.

At first, Kathleen was furious. In all the health and physical education classes she took in high school, no one talked about what *really* happened during pregnancy, and Kathleen had been truly shocked when she got so big. Off went her new engagement ring. She couldn't wear jewelry. Her breasts quickly dried up after she decided on formula, but they were denser and sagged. It often felt like she was lugging around two mounds of prickly, sometimes painful, beef. The doctors assured her that after the baby was born, her figure would shrink back down, which had happened for the most part—but the shape of her was not, and never would be, like before. The same thing had happened all over again with Nicholas.

Now, with the boys constantly at her heels, Kathleen had gotten used to hiding her body, and dressed herself every morning as quickly as possible. She avoided mirrors and sometimes even caught herself staring enviously at Virgil's physique. Where he had barely changed since college, Kathleen felt as though she were a constantly shifting landscape, inside and out. It was all so profoundly unfair.

In the bedroom, Kathleen lifted a heavy leg and shoved it into the suit. Then she did the other leg. She was prepared for failure, but to her delight—with some yanking and stretching—she worked the straps onto her shoulders and ran her hands down her middle, pleased at how well it smoothed everything out, then wrapped the towel around her waist and slipped her feet into a pair of old tennis sneakers. She shuffled toward the front door, grabbing her cigarettes and ashtray and the little transistor radio on the way out so she could listen to music.

Downstairs in the courtyard, it was a quiet morning. The apartments were empty. All the old folks were at church.

The water was clean, like it was ready for her. *It's blue as a dream*, she thought, toeing herself out of the sneakers.

She climbed the little metal stepladder down into the water, smooth and warmed by late autumn sunlight, and suddenly Kathleen Beckett was weightless.

Her body had always responded well to being outdoors, and this was one thing, at least, that hadn't changed. She swam a few lengths, then returned to the edge of the pool, admitting to herself that she had not felt this good in a long time. She anchored her toes on the bottom, then moved her knees, watching her legs create waves underwater. All thoughts about the woman's phone call, and what might come of it, disappeared. *Virgil will be back soon* was all she thought as she turned on the radio, and by the time she heard the Bluebird roll back into the carport from church, Kathleen had been listening to the news for over an hour, and knew what the Russians had done.

Sputnik 2 was in outer space, and on board were radio transmitters, telemetry systems, air-regeneration and temperature-control systems, two photometers measuring solar radiation and cosmic rays, and underneath the satellite, strapped into a small, cone-shaped pressurized cabin, rode a tiny dog called "Laika."

5.

Like almost every other outfit in the greater Wilmington area, Louviers Country Club was owned by DuPont. It operated exclusively for its employees, but Louis Porter had partnered with William duPont Jr. to build the Delaware Park horse track, so the agents at Equitable Life Insurance were welcome. It was a nice perk. Though the new job was a pay cut, Virgil got the golf membership out of it, and a brand-new robin's-egg 1957 Buick Bluebird.

It was not a car Virgil would have chosen for himself, but he understood it was part and parcel of what was expected of him in his new position, one that would demand actual door-to-door time. The Bluebird was a low-end, four-door hardtop sedan with whitewall tires, shiny chrome trim, and modest tail fins sharking out from the rear. Virgil had never owned a new car in his life. As he steered the Bluebird along the winding driveway that encircled the sprawling green lawns of Louviers, he enjoyed the gasoline smell of the matching blue vinyl seats. The tires made crunching sounds on the gravel.

It was noon on the dime.

He hadn't always played golf; he'd never golfed in Monterey, and made fun of his college friends who golfed at UD. Virgil liked to admit, somewhat pridefully, that he wasn't good at things he wasn't interested in, but it wasn't long out of college before he realized why they all golfed: at any business on the East Coast, Sunday golfing was de rigueur, and Virgil was forced to pick it up when he started at Manifest Insurance, the reason he and Kathleen had left Delaware and moved up to Pawtucket.

As with all else in Virgil Beckett's life thus far, the job at Manifest had just sort of worked out.

The spring before graduation, he had been following Kathleen around to her tennis matches when he realized that summer was coming, then fall, and he had made no plans of his own. When they decided to get married, his lack of prospects became a pressing matter. Walter Lovelace, Kathleen's father, had already passed from a cancer of the brain, but Virgil knew from what stories she shared that Walter, who taught courses at Wharton with titles like Inherited Wealth

Leadership and Managing the Emerging Enterprise, had been a man serious about words like "prospects." The world of business mystified Virgil, yet it was the environment from which his new wife had sprung, so when he saw an advertisement in the Wilmington *News Journal* for a job with an insurance company in Pawtucket offering "high earning potential," capitalism's most unlikely candidate entertained the idea of selling life insurance in Rhode Island.

Virgil had never been to the state. He imagined it was an actual island. He knew there were beaches there. He thought living in the Ocean State would be sort of like living in Monterey, so he sent in a brief query about the position and, within a week, had bought himself a well-loved '42 Nash and was shaking hands with his new work colleagues: Donald Frazier Jr., George Burpee, and George Stimp.

On his very first day at the office, the men asked him to join them golfing on Sunday.

Virgil, who thought Sundays were supposed to be a day off, hesitated. Besides not knowing how to golf, Virgil Beckett preferred to do nothing on his days off but lie on the couch with the paper spread over his chest, listening to Charlie Parker — but to his credit, he correctly intuited that the invitation was not exactly optional, and so he went.

It turned out golfing suited him.

Golf wasn't exercise. It was barely a sport. You spent the afternoon outdoors, leisurely strolling from hole to hole with teenage boys caddying, looking up to you, hoping you could give them a job one day. Virgil got the hang of the game fairly quickly, and it wasn't long before he began actually looking forward to, as his colleagues put it, "swinging wood" on Sundays.

As a bonus, Virgil liked Frazier, Burpee, and Stimp. The men didn't seem to work that hard, and were never in a bad mood. They all shared the same kind of smile. After Virgil landed his first client, they took him out for a steak at the Carriage Inn and Saloon thirty miles south in North Kingstown, an old stone cellar restaurant with a fireplace dating back almost two hundred years. They ordered drinks, talking about the return of the Olympic Games to London when the waiter was present, and some new book called *Sexual Behavior in the Human Male* when the waiter was not.

Several rounds of whiskey with egg whites and cherries later, Frazier told Virgil his ambition was fine and all but wasn't really necessary: his father, Donald Frazier Sr., "owned half of Rhode Island," he said, and the old man had promised his son that he would keep the business afloat in perpetuity. All of their clients were Don Sr.'s. Manifest Insurance was the one place in the world, Virgil's colleagues assured him, where a man didn't have to do "a damn thing." Frazier winked at him and lifted his glass. George Burpee did the same, and so did George Stimp. They all toasted one another, and Virgil lifted his glass and toasted them. He toasted himself.

He felt like he had won a lottery.

A few nights later, when the men started pushing him to accompany them for drinks at Crooly's after work, there was no question that Virgil would join them.

Crooly's Bar: an Irish pub no longer run by Irishmen. It was an odd choice, perhaps, Virgil thought, for three professional men in midlife, but after the war, when the mills closed, the nightlife in Pawtucket had quickly followed suit. A half-brick, half-shingle outlier, the place was basically a converted garage and had existed for years in an oily part of the city close to the Massachusetts border. Virgil learned that his trio of colleagues went there every Wednesday and Thursday night. Frazier, Burpee, and Stimp were well into their forties, and each had a family, Virgil knew, but they went to Crooly's despite—or perhaps because of—their marriages.

The first few times Virgil went to Crooly's, he drank so much that he threw up afterward in the alley, and had to retreat to the bar's dark little bathroom to clean himself up before going home to Kathleen. It wasn't long, though, before he built up a tolerance and soon was keeping pace with the other men, who seemed, to Virgil's genuine amazement, capable of drinking for hours without any visible effect at all. They were happy to have him at Crooly's, because if there was one talent Virgil Beckett possessed in the world, it was his ability to instantly procure female attention, anywhere he went. The first night he joined them, they told him they thought he was not merely handsome but *pretty*, and as he watched the men sweep up the women he rejected, Virgil wondered if that hadn't been their plan in hiring him all along.

So it had gone for nine years.

Then, one cold Monday morning last April, just days after Virgil broke it off with Little Mo, his colleagues took their secretary to a wet lunch for her birthday. Virgil, nursing the isolation of his newfound sobriety, stayed behind. When the phone rang in Frazier's office, he answered it.

An old man was on the line, talking about some balloon he wanted to buy. "A big silver balloon," he said. "Bigger than in a circus or parade and you will look up in the sky and it will be there!" The man—he sounded *very* old to Virgil—told him that he was tired of living alone, and wanted to come live with Don and his wife, Marilyn, and their girls, if they would have him. He wasn't eating right. Two days ago, he said, the electricity went out at the cottage, and nobody had come to fix it!

Shaken, Virgil said he had the wrong number, and hung up. For all these years, he thought, no one had said a word to him about Don Sr. being infirm.

Virgil kept his hand on the receiver longer than he meant to, and when it rang again, it startled him. He didn't answer. Instead, he started flipping through Frazier's Rolodex. A card he found said "Dad" on it, and revealed two addresses in Rhode Island. One was in Newport. The other was an address in Portsmouth, about thirty miles south. Don had added a note in pencil: *Common Sense Point (cottage).*

Virgil didn't know what made him go see Donald Frazier Sr. that day, but it was likely something to do with the fact that his own father had just moved out of Monterey and into a small shingled cabin in the Santa Lucia Mountains with a sweeping ocean view. It had only recently gotten a telephone. Aware of the landslides that often happened out there—one had taken out an early attempt at the Bixby Bridge—Virgil was worried about his father living alone.

Last year, when his sister Irenie married and moved with her machinist to someplace in Oregon, Virgil had tried to convince his father to move east, to come live with him and Kathleen, but Coke Beckett said he wasn't going *anywhere*. He'd been wanting to live in Big Sur ever since Bitsy died, he said, and flatly told Virgil that he'd rather a mudslide got him than live anywhere near the East Coast with its "drunks, snobs, and assholes." An honest death was better than a dishonest life, Coke liked to say. "Your mother's death was early," he often said, "but honest."

With the men out of the office, there was no one to complain when Virgil put on his coat and hat, hung the CLOSED sign, and left.

His Nash was in the shop, and Virgil had nearly frozen himself walking to work that morning, so he climbed into Frazier's black '55 Windsor in the parking lot. He caught the keys when they dropped from the visor and turned on the heat, full blast. He drove to a nearby filling station that offered free coffee, bought a fifteen-cent map of the state, and as he headed down I-95 through Providence, he thought about the day Coke had spoken with police about Bitsy.

They were trying to blame the bus driver, who was distraught but insistent that he'd had the right-of-way: "The woman just clean stepped out in front of me!" he cried, and Virgil, not yet fourteen, watched his father put up one flat hand as if to say: "No more." Coke didn't doubt the veracity of the bus driver's story for a *second*, he told the police, because his wife, though very beautiful and he loved her, *never* looked where she was going. "Elizabeth walked like she was Moses," he said, "expecting the whole damn world to part just for her." For years, Coke told them, he had yanked her off curbs, pulled her out of gutters, and Virgil knew his father was right. His mother used to laugh at her own absentmindedness: *"I'm such a dizzy doo!"* she liked to say, and it always made him scared. Like Bitsy, Virgil Beckett also often caught himself in a dreamy, fallen sort of state, and had spent a great deal of time worrying whether his mother's fate might not one day be his own. He could hold an entire conversation with Kathleen and not remember a word. Faces and names were lost to him. He had never slept in school, nor was he ever fully awake. And how many times had he been walking someplace and suddenly realized that he didn't know where he was? Or where he was going? It didn't seem at all unlikely that one day Virgil could accidentally step in front of a bus, off the edge of the world.

Two months after the accident, he went to the library, looked up Moses, and was comforted. If his mother walked like she was Moses, he thought, maybe it meant that she was seeing something no one else could see.

According to the map, it turned out that Common Sense Point was actually called Common *Fence* Point, and it occupied the upper tip of Aquidneck Island in Portsmouth. Tiverton was east, Newport due south, a place, Virgil had heard, filled with fifteen-room mansions offering the best kind of rocky Atlantic coast vistas. Four years ago, Senator John F. Kennedy and Jacqueline Bouvier had been married there, with a grand reception at the Auchincloss estate for twelve hundred guests. It was exactly the kind of place, he guessed, where a man who "owned half of Rhode Island" would live.

Virgil exited onto Route 195, then traveled down 114, past Barrington, Warren, and Bristol. To get to Portsmouth, he had to cross the Mount Hope Bridge, the longest suspension bridge in New England, and as he motored across it, he admired the towers that shot up into the sky, the way the suspension cables swooped and retreated. Bitsy had taken him to see the Golden Gate Bridge in '37, right after it opened, and he recalled walking down Market Street arm in arm with his mother that day, then along the Embarcadero with its trash and its seagulls.

She had been talking about the earthquake of 1906. She was five years old when it happened, but she remembered it all: Her family lost their home. Fled south to Monterey. "I met your father because of an earthquake," she said, and pointed out which buildings had burned, and been rebuilt. Smoke billowed into the air that day like a volcano, Bitsy said, and stopped walking when she told him how she could still feel the heat from the fires that seemed born out of the sky. She touched her cheeks. Ash was everywhere, she said, and choked your throat. Many people died, but people also helped one another, she said. That was the day, she told him, that she learned she was not afraid of dying.

At sunset, they drove to the bridge. Bitsy parked the car. "Let's walk across," she said, and pointed out the way for pedestrians.

"It's red," he said.

"Vermilion," said his mother.

He was eleven years old. The Becketts had never been religious, but as Virgil walked high above the Pacific Ocean underneath the bridge's gigantic red-orange towers, his childish imagination explained away the thrill he felt as God. His mother sang a cowboy song she liked, "There's a Silver Moon on the Golden Gate." It had commemorated the bridge's opening just two months before:

And it shines above on the one I love
Silvery charms caress the arms I'm longing for.

Virgil hummed the tune as he drove into and across the north end of Portsmouth. When a sign with a cow on it told him he had arrived in Common Fence Point, he navigated a narrow road until he reached the end of an odd, barren neck of land where apparently cattle once grazed.

He stopped the car.

This was not Newport. There were no mansions here. There were barely any houses. A dirt path smothered by seagrass led to an isolated cottage with a leaning front porch obscured by tribes of overgrown rosebushes. The cottage, gray shingled, was missing several shutters, and those that remained were all stripped of their paint. It looked not only like no one was home but that no one had visited the property for some time. Virgil opened the door of the Windsor and stepped outside, but the wind was so fiercely cold that he nearly gave up.

He'd come this far, he thought, and blew on his hands, stuffing them into his armpits as he approached the porch. He banged on the front door. Through the windows there was nothing but old furniture, so he walked around the cottage, into the rear yard.

An elderly man was resting himself on the stump of an oak tree.

"Mr. Frazier?" Virgil said. "Are you Mr. Frazier?"

The man was wearing one of those old-fashioned wool suits and a brown derby hat, as though about to embark for a day at the office in 1924. He appeared to Virgil to be staring at the bridge, its towers and cables quite visible in the sky from this distance, but his back had calcified into a monstrous posture. Virgil stepped closer. The man's hands were white and gripped his kneecaps. His mouth and chin, slunk into a frown, were slick, and the wool on his shoulders glistened with the dew of the Atlantic, carried by the wind off the bay.

Virgil stood in a wave of revulsion, wondering what to do, wondering how this could be the same man he had spoken with not an hour before. With no other feasible options, he returned to the car. He hurried to the mainland, reported what he'd seen to the police from a pay phone, then parked the Windsor in its space in the parking lot and did not return to Manifest Insurance again. Didn't even send a letter of resignation. (There was nothing, really, to resign from.)

It took two weeks, and he interviewed unsuccessfully at four different companies in Rhode Island before getting the idea to try Delaware, where Lou Porter and Artie Wooz at Equitable Insurance, who had never heard of Manifest but were pleased with his purported work experience, his UD pedigree, met and liked him.

Virgil steered the Bluebird into Louviers. He opened the trunk, gave his clubs to the attendant. After a quick change of clothes, he looked for, and easily found, the other men of Equitable. They were all climbing into golf carts out back.

Wooz saw him first, and waved.

"We'd left you for dead, Beckett!" he shouted.

"I'm here," Virgil said.

Artie Wooz was there with some friend of his from Yale. They rode together, and Lou Porter was riding with someone Virgil didn't know from DuPont.

The DuPont Experimental Station and the DuPont Hospital for Children next to Brandywine Creek collectively employed over eighty percent of the city. Louis Porter himself, Wooz said, had managed to insure over a third of DuPont employees. As soon as the old man retired, Wooz liked to boast, he had his sights set on signing all of them.

With the men paired off, Virgil climbed into a golf cart by himself, slightly annoyed. "Odd number?" he shouted.

Wooz pointed behind him. "Braddock's back," he said.

Virgil turned around.

Tom Braddock hadn't shown his face at Equitable in a month, not since his son William died.

Virgil steeled himself for it, wishing he were riding with Wooz. Or anyone. As Braddock approached, Virgil saw that the man had tried hard to put himself together: his chin was shaved, his hair was combed, his clothes were ironed. His shirt was tucked in, tight. But no order in his appearance could hide the suffering that haunted his face. On Braddock's left hand, there was no longer a wedding ring.

He slid into the seat next to Virgil. "Got everything?" he asked, tugging on a glove.

"I do," Virgil said. "So we're off."

The men took off in a line of golf carts, toward the tee. Occasionally, one of them would point at the sky. Autumn was over, and the tall, pale firs stood full against the bare spindles of the maples and oaks. Despite the heat, somehow Virgil could smell winter coming. After living on the East Coast for twelve years, he still hadn't gotten used to the rhythm of the changing seasons, how every four months, the whole world looked brand-new.

"How's Sally doing?" he asked, once he remembered the name of Braddock's wife.

Tom didn't answer. "They sent another one up," he said. "Did you hear?"

Virgil nodded. "*Sputnik 2*," he said. "They put a dog in there, in a capsule in the rocket. They're calling her 'Muttnik.' Isn't that something?"

"It's stupid and cruel," Tom said. "Killing an animal like that. Poor dog is above us right now, burning up in outer space."

Here was a dead man for you, Virgil thought.

"So you're from the West Coast," Tom said.

"Monterey," Virgil said.

Tom looked back at him brightly. "Like Steinbeck," he said. "*Cannery Row* territory."

"That's right," Virgil said. He knew the book, of course, but his family had always made it a point to avoid the sardine district growing up. It really stank there.

"Reading is all I can do these days," Tom said. "I'm thinking about writing a book about Japan in 1868, during the fall of the shogunate."

Virgil didn't know what he was expected to say to that. It sounded like another death in the family.

"There used to be lots of Japanese in Monterey," he said. "Before the war. My father says there aren't too many there now, though. Japs."

A black groundskeeper crossed the green in a lawnmower the size of a small car. When Virgil looked closer, he realized it *was* a car, a stripped vintage Ford outfitted with a gang of five single mowers dragging behind it.

"You were in Rhode Island before us, is that right?" Tom asked.

"Pawtucket," Virgil said.

"How long were you there?"

"About nine years."

"Why'd you leave?"

They parked the cart. Virgil watched the caddies unloading their clubs. The Canada geese were there, had landed at the first tee. Everyone was laughing. The caddies, all local teenagers, were drawing out golf clubs like swords and running through the birds, forcing them back into the sky.

"A change of scenery," he said.

Tom nodded. "I won't be here much longer. I can't stand it. I've been trying to get Sally to move the boys, get a fresh start. But she won't ever leave Wilmington."

As Virgil's caddy handed him the driver to tee off, a rebellious parking attendant started blasting the song "Jailhouse Rock" from a car radio.

He was taking Kathleen to see the new Elvis movie on Friday. Even though Virgil hated Elvis and his music in a way he didn't know was possible to hate another human being, Kathleen seemed to like him, and she'd loved that Judy Tyler movie they saw over the summer. Leaving the theater, she'd leaned her head on his shoulder and told him what a great night she'd had, so he promised her that they would go.

He was trying.

One night last month, when he got home from work, he opened the record player in the living room, dropped the needle on their song, and went to look for his wife.

Kathleen was in the bedroom, holding up her old tennis dress over her figure, the one she was wearing in the photograph hanging in Memorial Library. Her racquet, the Dunlop Gold Wing, was on their bed.

Virgil leaned against the doorjamb and folded his arms. "Put it on," he said.

Kathy threw it at him and laughed. "Fat chance," she said.

He folded the dress in half and dropped it on a chair. He stuck out a hand. "Dance with me," he said.

It was October 3rd at seven in the evening. The boys were

outside, with the Parousia boys. Tomorrow, William Braddock would have a heart attack on his father's front lawn and the first *Sputnik* would scream into space, but in that moment, together, Virgil and Kathleen glided into the living room of 14B and slow-danced in a way they hadn't since college. Virgil felt his wife's body relax as they danced, her legs moving in and out of his own. Because of Ruth, Kathleen was a good dancer. Her back arched a little when he moved his hand up her arm with two fingers. He kissed her neck, ran his lips up one ear. *"You are the angel glow that lights a star,"* he sang, *"the dearest things I know are what you are."*

"Faker," she whispered, and smiled.

6.

They had been living at Acropolis Place for over six months. For over six months, Kathleen had been listening to the sound of the Bluebird pulling into the carport. It was the little things, she knew by now, the small repetitions, that made a life. This morning Kathleen slowly drifted from one end of the pool to the other. She rested her back against the coping and lit a cigarette that she did not plan to smoke as she listened to her family walk up the stairs in silence, to Virgil opening the door to 14B. She heard her husband calling her name, and when Nathaniel first stepped out onto the balcony, she looked up at her eldest son—his long limbs, his brown hair and angular shoulders—and thought what she so often thought when she saw him: *What is past is past.*

Nicholas, cartoonishly shorter than Nathaniel, though only one year behind him, grabbed on to the balcony railing next to his brother.

"Mother's in the pool!" he cried.

You could not go back. Kathleen had talked herself through it so many times, and was still unable to say for certain what happened. She didn't see Billy Blasko in college—but she had seen him once after college, in the fall of '48, just three months after she married Virgil Beckett and moved to Pawtucket.

Mrs. Beckett had held entire conversations in her mind, with judge and jury, about what she had done, the right and wrong of it, and had always, every time, concluded that Nathaniel was no one's business but her own. Her decision to say yes to Virgil had meant saying no to tennis, and at the time, Kathleen thought she would have been a good tennis player; she was not entirely confident that she could have been great.

She had believed Randy Roman at first, the tennis scout who said he could make her famous, that scrawny, oddly complacent man from Brooklyn who told Kathleen several times during her senior year of college that she had Wimbledon "in her pocket," who said he'd be her manager, travel the country with her—and if she did well here, Australia—right up to the moment he slid his hand around her bottom and squeezed. Kathleen turned down Randy Roman not because she loved Virgil Beckett more than tennis but because she hated losing.

The Most

Margaret Osborne duPont was the greatest female player in the world, she also lived in Wilmington, and Kathleen started wondering how many tennis champions one city could contain. As soon as Mr. Roman's hand swept itself across her ass, she suddenly could not trust that she would ever actually beat the record of Margaret Osborne duPont. Marrying Virgil, she thought, was the safer bet. Maybe she couldn't win, but she wouldn't lose.

It wasn't long before Kathleen worried she'd made a mistake. Virgil had taken the first job he found. Kathleen knew he was lazy, but he didn't even *try*.

The job was what Walter Lovelace would have called "a low-class operation" with some obscure insurance company in, of all places, Pawtucket, Rhode Island. Kathleen had visited the state once before, for a match at Brown. When she heard what Virgil had done, when he told her they would be moving to Rhode Island, she kidded herself remembering the nice restaurants in the Armory District, the field trip the tennis team had taken to the Providence Athenaeum. Her major at UD was English language arts, and Kathleen had seen up close and in person first editions of Poe, Whitman, and as she stood in the vast collections, smelling the aging leaves of poems, they felt like sacraments. Along with his letters, Billy had often sent Kathleen books to read, all of which she kept displayed on her bookshelves. He told her about Czechoslovakian writers he loved with unpronounceable names: Hašek, Kukučín, Cíger-Hronský—Kathleen had started every book that Billy ever sent.

In June of '48, after the wedding, when Virgil and Kathleen had packed up their trunks at UD and driven the three hundred miles from Newark up to Pawtucket, neither one was prepared for what awaited them. They arrived on a cloudy day, and the imprint made itself early and strong: Pawtucket's textile and iron factories had either closed or moved south during the Depression, the war, where labor was cheaper. All of the workers lost their jobs.

Virgil and Kathleen's new home on Bend Street sat across the river from the old Slater cotton mill.

Kathleen told herself not to be a snob; she knew her husband didn't know about money. When Ruth died, Kathleen learned from the lawyer that Walter Lovelace had changed his will, donating the bulk of his savings, including the family mansard in the Highlands and all of its contents, to a charity for veterans upon Ruth's passing, leaving Kathleen with only a small cash inheritance. Despite what had happened between them, Kathleen was not bitter. It was more than enough for a down payment on a reasonable mortgage, and she told Virgil that he should be the one to pick out the house.

The house Virgil chose was the appropriate size for a young couple, and had been newly painted buttercup yellow with white trim. It was attractive, Kathleen admitted, with a peaked roof, and a brick chimney for a fireplace that took up most of one side of the living room. There was a wraparound yard in decent shape, and a mature oak tree stood in the yard, near the front door. The problem was the neighborhood. Their house was one of the lone singles. The rest of Bend Street was apartment buildings filled with the anguished cries of unemployed tenants.

That first evening in Pawtucket, they went for a walk. Virgil, sensing in Kathleen some doubt, put his arm around her shoulders and pointed out mansards and Victorians on nearby streets Walnut and Walcott, with their lush green gardens. "This is the good life," he said, and Kathleen didn't know whether he meant now or later.

The small yellow house got no light, and there wasn't a working bulb in the place. While Virgil started at Manifest, Kathleen spent hours in the company of a mop, bucket, and broom, wiping away cobwebs, scrubbing every greasy, dismal corner. The kitchen, especially, was in an appalling state, with the back of the icebox draped in black mold. Mice droppings filled the food cabinets, and their furry cadavers awaited her in the basement, along with some horrible slime creeping up the foundation, as though the earth were trying to pull down the house with several hands. The bathroom, trimmed in pink-and-black tile, was oversized, bigger than one of the bedrooms, and the tub was stained orange from iron residue in the public water.

At least the place was quick to organize. The furniture they ordered arrived, the phone line got connected. There was a local women's sports club, which Kathleen immediately joined, but the other women all had children already, of various ages, and she found it was all they would talk about.

It was the intensity of her isolation that surprised her, a painful return to all she had known as a child. With little else to do, Kathleen Beckett found herself dreaming about Kathleen Lovelace, winner of multiple Grand Slam singles, an identical twin living an alternate life, traveling the world with a real manager, posing for photographers, beating out Margaret Osborne duPont on the grass in front of a crowd of thousands at Wimbledon.

As the weeks passed, Kathleen could feel, in a literal, physical way, her talent ebbing out of her body. She was surprised to learn that muscles grew sore from disuse. The women at the club complimented her figure. She felt crazy.

When she learned from the butcher that the Pawtucket city planners were building Interstate 95 not four blocks from where they lived, Kathleen spent an entire afternoon crying upstairs in the bedroom.

Respite came only with Virgil's nightly return. On Kathleen's prompting, the two of them made a habit of going for long walks in the late evening that summer, and they started discussing things: how they came to be where they were, what they were grateful for. How they were better off in Pawtucket than being stuck in Newark like their friends. Mostly they amused themselves making fun of the characters they saw on the streets, and Virgil did an imitation of a drunk man that always killed her. One afternoon, for fun, Kathleen put her raincoat on over her nightgown and studied herself in a mirror. She started laughing. She thought she *actually* looked like one of the crazy characters. Emma Bovary in Pawtucket. Bertha Mason. What wife in literature, she thought, *wasn't* sick or insane, so she messed up her hair, slid her lipstick on wrong, and then, tickled by her disguise, she walked outside, crossing the Exchange Street bridge, to the offices of the Manifest Insurance Company.

Manifest was housed in a one-story brick building on High Street, next to an electrical supplies store, and a few streets down from the public library. She had been to the building once before, to meet Virgil's colleagues, none of whom, as far as Kathleen could discern, displayed a single remarkable quality.

Inside, there were four modest offices, and a pathetic little reception area with a single front desk was decorated with a wan-looking girl chewing gum. When Kathleen entered through the front door, the girl looked up from filing her nails.

Kathleen winked at her and put a finger to her lips. "*I'm Virgil's wife*," she whispered.

The girl rolled her eyes down Kathleen's body, then pointed her nail file in the direction of his office. Kathleen went to the door and opened it.

"Love me!" she shouted, and burst out laughing.

Virgil jumped out of his chair like someone shot him.

"Kathy, what the *hell*," he said. "You *walked* here like this?"

He ushered Kathleen to the parking lot, put her in the front seat of their Nash, then drove her the short distance back to Bend Street. He dropped her off, in front of their house, without a word.

It was September of 1948. They had been married three months, known each other not yet four years.

The next morning, Kathleen sat down to write Billy. She hoped that he was still living at the same address in Wilmington.

She told him she had graduated UD, married Virgil, and moved up to Rhode Island. She had kept all the books he'd sent her in college, she wrote, and was still playing tennis when she could, but wasn't competing anymore. She had not forgotten him, she said, and hoped they could see each other soon. She paused for a moment, then wrote without further hesitation, *Virgil works late Wednesdays and Thursdays.*

It wasn't a long letter, and she did not include her phone number, but Billy would have her new address on the envelope when he got it.

The second it dropped from her hands into the mail slot at the post office, Kathleen knew what would happen, and was not a bit surprised when, late Wednesday morning of the following week, a strange car pulled up in front of the house, and parked.

Kathleen darted into the bedroom and removed her housecoat. She put on a new green dress with a trapezoid bodice.

When the doorbell rang, she checked her face, then carried herself upright to answer it.

It had been six years. Having just turned twenty-two, Kathleen could only imagine what she looked like to him, as to her, Billy Blasko had completely changed. He was wearing a suit. There, in her doorway, were the eyebrows she remembered, with the same sunken eyes, but his sad expression had cemented into austerity, and his floppy hair was gone. Cut short. He was an American. As they stared at each other, Kathleen blushed, angry with herself for some unknowable reason—maybe for having waited so long to see him—and she momentarily panicked that this was a terrible idea, that maybe she didn't know this man at all, until Billy lifted his hand and placed it on her shoulder. He moved his palm down the side of her arm exactly as he had done the first day he kissed her, and Kathleen was suddenly charged with the knowledge that Virgil's hands had always moved up her body while Billy's had always moved down, and in that moment, she knew what she preferred.

Kathleen invited him into the living room. She showed him the bookshelf next to the fireplace where she kept all the books he sent her.

Billy did not look at the books. "I'm here," he said, and tugged her over to the sofa.

Neither mentioned it, but they both sat down understanding at once that her new marriage was simply irrelevant. Kathleen did not ask if Billy was married, but saw no ring. She wondered if he might have taken it off. He had lost his entire family in the war, he said. Elena and Ana. Their parents. Their grandparents. The cousins. Everyone was gone. "Mine too," said Kathleen. "My family is gone." The bridge in his hometown that he had told her about, the one that had been blown up and then repaired, had been bombed again. This time, no one knew when, or if, it would ever be fixed.

Billy Blasko stayed until four thirty in the afternoon. It was all the time they had but all they needed, as they both knew what it meant that he had come to see her.

Back in the summer of '42, Billy had taught Kathleen a final tennis move. He called it "The Most." In Czech, he said, the word *most* meant "bridge." Then he asked her what a bridge does.

"I know what a *bridge* is, knucklehead," she said.

"That's not what I asked. What does a bridge do?"

Kathleen stared at him. "It *covers water.*"

"A bridge is a passage, yes," he said, "but it is also a trap."

He told her to pick up her racquet.

There were people trapped on the bridge when it was destroyed, Billy's father had told him. People who died just walking home. In their honor, he had invented this tennis maneuver. You couldn't use it often, Billy said, because if you used it too often, it could be copied or predicted, but when deployed, The Most had brought Petr Blaško victory in every match he'd ever played.

Billy told Kathleen to stand at the center of the baseline, then he walked around the court to the other side. They started to volley.

As they played, everything was normal for a few minutes. Gradually, though, Kathleen felt the length of Billy's shots tighten. He was "ghosting," bringing her closer to the net while she was focused on the ball, and suddenly she was locked in. "We're on the bridge!" he shouted, and when they were just a few meters apart in constant volley, the net tall between them, Billy asked if she was ready. She nodded.

"Bomb's about to go off," he said, and tilted his racquet a funny way.

The ball flew at her, hard and fast, and Kathleen realized that her arm couldn't move in the direction she wanted it to.

She somehow sent the ball back, and Billy, anticipating its direction, sliced.

The ball soared out of reach, landing smartly in the corner of Kathleen's left service box.

Kathleen had used The Most sparingly. Only when she needed it. It's what brought her to victory in the final tournaments of both '47 and '48, and that afternoon, as Billy unzipped her dress on her new living room couch in Pawtucket, slid his warm hands down her bare back, she understood what was really going on: that by following Billy Blasko wherever he was about to go, there was a chance she would not, or could not, go home again.

7.

rtie Wooz won, of course. Wooz won almost every Sunday, and usually Virgil could not have cared less. What he liked about golf was that it never really seemed to matter who won; the point was to be outside in the sunshine, relaxing. But this time the other fellows at Equitable slapped Wooz's back and made a big deal about it. "When *Porter's* out of the picture," Virgil heard Wooz's friend from Yale murmur, and was frankly disgusted at the way the man made a choking motion with his hands and winked.

Otherwise, all the men talked about was *Sputnik 2*. The

DuPont fellow riding with Lou Porter had been contacted, he told the insurance agents, about working on the American space program. Their first industry-based research-and-development laboratory was already underway, building American rockets to send an American man into space. The insurance agents countered: Who wouldn't want to buy *life* insurance when the Russians had just sent half a ton of metal into space?

Virgil turned his mind to the parking lot. In his haste this morning, he had forgotten to check the lock of the trunk of the Bluebird.

Agents at Equitable were often gifted small items of appreciation from their clients, toiletry travel kits or tickets to movies, but as Virgil had yet to sign a single client, he was surprised two days ago when Alice Beth, their twenty-year-old secretary, buzzed to say there was a package for him that he had to sign for. He went to her desk, where the deliveryman handed over a long black case.

"What is it," Alice Beth asked.

He told her he didn't know. He clicked open the lid.

A saxophone glowed like some kind of relic.

Alice Beth clapped her hands in a way that made Virgil uneasy. "Ooooh!" she gushed. "Do you play?"

As a teenager in the years following Bitsy's death, Virgil had continued doing what he always did in Monterey: fishing, swimming. Mostly he did nothing at all. His sisters, Sarah, Rose, and Irenie, took care of all the shopping and cooking and cleaning, so he had nothing to forget to do. Because of his looks, everyone assumed he was a surfer, but he was not a surfer (the one time Virgil Beckett tried surfing, he fell off the board within ten seconds, was pummeled by a wave, and swallowed so much seawater that he was sick for two days)—but he liked spreading a blanket out on Del Monte Beach to watch the surfers ride and split waves. Saturday nights, he collected thirty-five cents and went to the movies.

In early May of '44, right before departing for Italy, Virgil went to see *Gaslight*, the new Bergman picture, at the Golden State Theatre on Alvarado. He was really going to watch the cartoons (Daffy Duck was his favorite), but when he got there, the movie was canceled. Instead there was a live bebop quartet featuring the saxophonist Charlie Parker.

With nothing else to do, Virgil decided to stay.

The theater was enormous, with a grand lobby and mezzanine, and could seat well over a thousand. Virgil counted the cigarettes of maybe forty people in the audience before the lights went down, and a lone spotlight appeared, following the musicians as they walked to the center of the stage.

Charlie Parker was the alto sax, Dizzy Gillespie was trumpet, and the names of the men playing piano and bass, Virgil didn't get.

Charlie Parker was wearing a blue-and-yellow-striped dinner jacket, a red polka-dot tie, and a gold chain for a neck strap. The white announcer stepped up to the microphone and explained to the audience that because of the ongoing musicians' strike against record companies, the session would not be recorded. What the audience was about to hear, he said, would be a "one-time thing," and repeated himself: what they heard tonight would *never be heard again*. Did everyone understand? The man had barely finished speaking when the music began. Virgil saw other people in the audience closing their eyes, so he closed his eyes.

The sound—how could you explain it? Virgil couldn't believe two hours had passed when the music stopped and the announcer walked back onstage. He went to the microphone and asked Charlie Parker how he got to be so good.

"Don't play the saxophone, let it play you," Charlie Parker said, and Virgil decided, then and there, that when he got back from Europe—if he got back—he would go to college and study the saxophone. To do it, he would have to get serious; leave Monterey and his dead mother far behind him. He would go east. Somewhere close to New York, he hoped.

He leaned over to a man sitting near him in the theater and tested a lie: "I play the saxophone," he said.

Standing in the reception area of the Equitable Insurance Company of Wilmington, Delaware, Virgil picked up the instrument. He had never held one before, and discovered it was heavy. He put his mouth around the mouthpiece and felt the strange slimness of the reed. His bottom lip pressed against his teeth. It felt like he was at the doctor, having his temperature taken with a gigantic golden thermometer. He put one hand inside the case and swept the velvet with his palm.

"No," he said to Alice Beth. "No, I don't."

"I guess you'll have to learn," Alice Beth said, and went back to typing.

Virgil carried the saxophone into his office and set it down on his desk. He stared at it. Then he picked it up again, placed the mouthpiece in his mouth, and tried to make a sound. Warm air moved through the instrument and puffed out the bell with a gassy smell. The reed was dry and left a chemical taste on his tongue. Virgil returned the instrument to its case, embarrassed. He didn't even know how to blow.

It was not a gift from a client, and it was certainly not from Kathleen, but all the hours he'd spent at Crooly's? Every man there had told the waitresses their dreams.

Virgil did not realize how much he'd confessed to Little Mo, but for years he'd talked openly at the bar, with boozy confidence, about moving back to Monterey one day, finding a little house somewhere by the ocean, and doing nothing but playing the saxophone. Why *couldn't* a man do nothing but play the sax and *be himself, be free*, he'd said. After all, it worked out for Charlie Parker.

When he told this to Little Mo, she punched him on the shoulder. "Bird died, dummy."

Virgil looked at her, shocked. "What? How?"

"I heard it was drugs," Little Mo said. "It was a couple years ago."

Virgil ordered a whiskey double and left the bar deeply hurt. He couldn't believe he hadn't known, and was irrationally upset that no one had told him. He walked through the back room, where there was an infamously tilted pool table and an old leather couch, and opened the rear entrance to Crooly's to get some air on the stoop. He was disconsolate, and wanted to feel that way by himself, but Little Mo followed him. She placed one arm around his shoulders and leaned her head into his neck. She kissed it.

Later that night on the couch, after they'd slept together, Virgil did something spontaneous. It was stupid, really, and clearly not serious, but he asked her to promise him that she would come back with him to California. It might be a while, he said, but he would think about her every day until they could. In jest, lying together, naked limbs entwined, he took one of Little Mo's tiny hands and, in a sloppy British accent that came out of nowhere, said: "Will you marry me, Miss Imogene Monson?"

She said she would marry him any day of the week.

He laughed, kissing her knuckles. "First," he said, grinning, "I gotta learn how to play the saxophone."

At his desk at Equitable, Virgil studied the case. He'd heard of Martins. He'd heard of Selmers and Conns—Charlie Parker had played a Conn. The saxophone Little Mo had sent him was a Jolly Frank, with a logo of a smiling rooster etched onto the bell. It was used, and up close Virgil could see that it was in pretty rough shape. He doubted it cost much, but a lot, perhaps, for a cocktail waitress. He would have to either return it to her or find some way to pay her back, because Virgil Beckett knew full well what it would mean to keep it. The woman might do something reckless. She could call him at home. Show up at his house.

Little Mo was in Pawtucket, and Kathleen was in Newark,

but the two cities were not far enough apart to give him comfort.

Virgil snapped the case shut and carried it outside to the Bluebird. He opened the trunk. He would keep the saxophone in the trunk of the Bluebird over the weekend, he thought, or until he knew what to do with it, so that was where the saxophone had resided when he drove the boys to church this morning, and while he golfed at Louviers.

As soon as Virgil's car was returned to him by the parking attendant, he checked the trunk and was relieved to discover that he hadn't forgotten to lock it after all. He said his goodbyes without shaking hands, without changing clothes. He was the first to depart. It was just four o'clock but somehow felt later. He didn't know what Kathleen was making for dinner, but he didn't care. Virgil found himself looking forward to their Sunday evening routine: Kathleen would bring Mrs. Donovan her dinner, she would serve the boys, then they would eat alone while the boys watched TV. Afterward, while Kathy cleaned up, Virgil would remove his shoes and lie on the sofa and watch with them. Sometimes Nicholas climbed on top of him and fell asleep on his chest.

Virgil pulled into the carport at Acropolis Place and turned off the engine. He would leave his golf bag in the back seat for now, he was thinking, while he went upstairs to 14B to check on everyone, when he glanced at the swimming pool and saw the blue towel. It hadn't moved from its spot by the pool cover. His wife's head was resting upon one raised shoulder.

Kathleen was still in the water.

The sun had by now nearly crossed over the pentagon of apartments. The yard and pool were almost in shadow. Virgil opened the door and got out of the car.

"Kathy!" he shouted.

She did not turn around to look at him when she said, "You're back."

Virgil walked to the edge of the pool. He looked down at his wife. "What's going on? What are you doing?"

Kathleen's hair had settled around her face in a wispy nest. Her skin had gone pale since the morning, and puffy. Her face and shoulders were swollen. Virgil watched her perform an odd trick: she set the base of her cranium so it rested on the coping, then, using her neck as the fulcrum this way, she bore the full weight of her entire body, which suddenly rose to the surface of the pool like a floating corpse.

"What do you mean?" she asked.

"Kathy, my God, have you been in here all this time? Where are the boys?"

"They're at Cosmo's."

Virgil dropped himself next to her. He gripped the edge of the pool. "Jesus, Kathleen. Honey. You really have to get out."

"I feel perfectly fine," she said. "Marvelous, actually. I don't know why we don't use the pool—it's just the best thing."

Kathleen rolled her body slowly from one side to the other, creating small waves. "I forgot to tell you. Your father called earlier."

Above them, behind the sliding glass doors, people were turning on the lights in their apartments, drinking cocktails, preparing dinner. A TV was already on in 10B. In 3C, Mrs. Donovan was no longer looking at the pool, but her silhouette slowly crossed the living room to the kitchen and back again. From 1A, Cosmo's unit, he heard Nicholas arguing with one of the Parousia boys about who was better, Russians or Americans.

"Okay, I'll be right back," he said. "I'm just going to call him back."

"Suit yourself," said Kathleen.

Virgil walked over to the Bluebird, yanked his clubs from the rear seat, then hurried upstairs to 14B and entered the apartment. He grabbed the phone receiver and thrust a finger in the dial. He knew the number for California by heart. On Sundays, he usually spoke with his father while Kathleen cooked dinner. All Coke Beckett ever wanted was to tell someone a story, and Virgil tried to indulge him as often as he could, but he had also accepted the fact that as his father grew older, his stories were changing:

Virgil didn't doubt that Coke fought in the Great War, but one day it was finding a blackened, severed human foot in the road with the shoe still on it, and the next it was an arm, cut off at the elbow, still wearing a glove. Coke had watched a cat eat the intestines from a soldier's gutted torso, he said. Then it was two coyotes, fighting over the soldier's bloody, fist-sized heart. Coke said he found himself face-to-face with a German, bayonets each at the ready, but Coke was faster, and thrust his bayonet into the man's side, twisting until the purple liver was showing. The following week he said he never used a bayonet at all. He never needed it. The only time he'd ever killed a man, he said, he used "these," and held up his arthritic, crooked hands. Coke had dozens of stories, and Virgil didn't know if they were changing because they were lies or because they were truths.

After Bitsy died, when Virgil went to the library in Monterey to look up Moses, he'd also asked the librarian about his father's movie, *The Dubious Few*. He thought he might track down a reel. The librarian went to the catalogues and looked it up. There was no record of it. But that didn't mean, she said, that it didn't exist.

Virgil listened to Coke answer the phone. "Dad," he said. "It's me. Kathleen said you called."

"I didn't call anybody. Is she there? In the room?"

Virgil squeezed the receiver between his neck and shoulder, extending the cord into the kitchen. For the second time today, he made for the tub of White Colonel. While sipping a large pour that he felt he deserved, he watched from the kitchen window as the last of the sunlight slipped off the roof of the pentagon, leaving Kathy's pool in darkness.

"You didn't call?" he said. "Kathleen says you called."

"That woman," he said, "is a liar."

"Dad, what are you talking about?"

His father coughed. "Did you hear? They sent up another one. They've got a dog up there."

"I heard," said Virgil.

"You think I'm nuts."

"Nobody thinks that," Virgil said, and heard him rustling through papers. "Dad."

"At least I married a woman who loved me," said Coke. "I knew the second I saw that boy. I *knew* it!"

"Knew *what?*"

"He's not your son," his father said.

Virgil rested his glass on the counter. "What are you talking about, Colson."

"I've got the proof right here! I've got the blood work back. I got the results of his type. Nathaniel is type A and you are type B. That boy is *not* your child."

"Dad," Virgil said, shaking his head. "I don't think it works like that. You're not making any sense."

"Ask her! She has to be A or AB, and AB is the rarest one. Pretty much nobody has AB. Ask her what type she is, then you call me back."

"Wait a second—"

Coke laughed. "*I'm* not the one not making sense. I married an honest woman!"

"Dad!"

He wasn't there.

Virgil listened to the dial tone, then hung up and thought: *Christ.* Coke had never been a fan of Kathleen's, and Virgil had never understood why. First he thought it was because of her looks—Kathleen Lovelace, his father always reminded him, was no Bitsy Beckett—but that wasn't it. After Nathaniel was born, and even though he had just made the trip in '48, to attend their wedding, Coke crossed the country to come to Pawtucket and see the baby. The arguing started the first evening he arrived on Bend Street and didn't stop until he left. His father had picked on Kathleen about everything. The food she served, how the house was kept. Once, after Coke complained that her rice pudding was watery, Virgil grabbed his father by the wrist and told him: "Colson Beckett, if you don't keep quiet, I will ask you to leave and not come back."

Coke had looked at his arm, and then his son. He pressed his mouth into a line. *"Get your house in order,"* he seethed.

Virgil, who had not gone a single time to Crooly's while his father was visiting, racked his brain, trying to understand how his father could have known about it. *All those girls.* Somehow, though, he *must* have known, and if so, Virgil found it deeply unfair of Coke to take Virgil's indiscretions, dalliances—if that's what you could call them—out on his wife.

After Coke finally left, he and Kathleen were so relieved to have him gone that Virgil forgot to worry about what might have set him off in the first place.

It was almost four thirty. Evening had arrived in the late afternoon, like it always did in November, and Virgil walked out onto the balcony. In the darkened pool below, Kathleen was swimming. Virgil watched her take a few laps. His boys were out of sight. He hadn't married the wrong woman, he thought; she married the wrong man. Virgil Beckett had eased himself into a job that almost destroyed him. Slept with pretty much any willing woman.

It was a myth that handsome men were only interested in beautiful women: Virgil Beckett was not picky at all. Sex, for him, was an act of vanity, and as he watched Kathleen swim, it occurred to him with shocking clarity that he could have, and probably should have, married another woman very easily.

It wasn't a matter of right or wrong: a man as pretty as Virgil was bound to have no feminine equal. It was different for his mother; Bitsy must have known from a young age that her beauty would be her sole asset in life, and for reasons mysterious to Virgil, Colson Beckett, who would love his ditzy, stunning wife right up to the moment she walked smack in front of that bus, had been deemed worthy of receiving it. A man did not need to be pretty for a pretty woman to be worthy of him, but the rules changed for Virgil: you really could be *too pretty* as a man. Whatever poor woman agreed to marry him would suffer a lifetime feeling—less than. Virgil was seeing it more and more in Kathleen. It had not escaped him, the way she protected her body from view when they changed in the bedroom. The net of age, they both knew, had caught her. Her hips, waist, and face were all spreading. But the widening of Kathleen was something Virgil truly could not have cared less about. It was the way she looked at his body with scorn, with jealousy, that made him resent her. He leaned over the balcony. "Coke said he never called," he shouted.

"Oh, he called, all right," Kathleen shouted back, as Nicholas and Nathaniel sprinted out from the front door of 1A and made for the stairs.

It was almost dinnertime. Through the open windows of other apartments, warm winds of fried chicken and pork chops circulated the pentagon. Someone was making a Sunday roast. Virgil wondered whether Kathleen planned on leaving the pool to do anything about it, or whether they would have to go out.

The Beckett family had gone out for dinner once in Newark

to Mr. Chop Stick, a Chinese restaurant where nothing was Chinese, Kathleen had said, except the waiters with their appallingly insincere grins. They put sugar in everything, and Nicholas had found what he was convinced was a chicken toe in his lo mein, and refused to ever go there again. The only other option nearby was Rudy's Drive-Up, a place that barely counted as dinner. Roller waitresses skated to your car and took orders, and you ate fried food on trays. The place was packed with teenagers.

Nicholas and Nathaniel opened the door to 14B and made straight for the TV without speaking to their father. They turned it on.

"We haven't eaten yet. Is that a good idea?" Virgil said.

"We're watching *You Asked for It*," said Nicholas, as though he were obeying the only law that ever was.

Virgil didn't like the show, where viewers wrote in asking to see something reenacted on television. He was hardly a prude, but he caught the boys last week watching pinup models in bikinis doing basic math, and thought it was indecent. It was strange; it wouldn't have been, he thought, if you saw it in person. There was something about the television that made it indecent.

"I'm going to talk to your mother," he told them. "Stay put."

The boys, bellies flat on the carpet, inches from the TV screen, weren't going anywhere.

Both Nicholas and Nathaniel seemed to like Newark, and Virgil was glad about it. The school was better than their old one, they had told him, and there were better sports. Both of his sons were serious and organized about their play in a way that Virgil never had been. Nicholas, though short, had the better overall build, and Virgil could imagine him wrestling one day, if he wanted. He didn't know what Nathaniel would do, but knew his eldest son loved him, and occasionally admired him. No one else in the house liked his music, but whenever he lay down on the sofa to listen to jazz, the boy would sit at the other end, resting a book on his father's feet.

Virgil stared at the back of Nathaniel as he watched TV. He was going to be tall, like Kathleen. The boy's lean, eight-year-old calves were already beginning to take shape. His brown hair sat in a small pile on top of his head. Virgil did not understand what Coke was on about. Nicholas had *always* looked like Bitsy and Nathaniel had *always* looked like Kathleen.

Dementia, Virgil thought, with a sinking feeling, and shook the image of Donald Frazier Sr.'s body slumped over that tree stump out of his head. "*A big silver balloon,*" the old man had said. "*You will look up in the sky and it will be there.*"

8.

cropolis Place Apartments," Kathleen Beckett had read in the pamphlet. "Your dream home on a hill! A *modern* home for the *modern* family," and in it were color pictures of a white family at ease: Father, a pipe in his mouth, sitting on the couch with a newspaper unfolded over his lap like a blanket — two children, boy and girl, playing at his feet — and Mother perched comfortably on one of the armrests, watching over them with a congenial smile. Behind her, a gleaming new tri-stationed kitchen offering "abundant counter and storage space for the work of meal making," and in the background, outside, through the sliding glass door, young neighbors waved from their wrought-iron balconies, the long fins of gleaming new cars were parked in their gleaming new carports, and at the center of it all, surrounded by grass, was a narrow concrete path leading up to and around a glistening, kidney-shaped, turquoise-blue community swimming pool.

Acropolis Place, Kathleen thought while the hours slipped by. How was she to have known it was a dingy apartment complex filled with old people? The day they arrived, they'd carried their belongings past an ambulance there to service a pair of kindly octogenarians who had each taken a fall. The moment Kathleen entered 14B and glanced at the sad little kitchen, the green wall-to-wall carpet with a stain next to the fireplace, it was evident to her, if to no one else in the family, that death now surrounded them.

The only good news was the pool. Everyone had been excited to use it. The day they arrived, the boys stood on the balcony, pointing, asking their mother when they could swim.

But the pool was covered, sealed for winter.

Kathleen checked in on her college friends who had remained in the area and lived close to one another in York-towne. Patricia said she would try to call on Kathleen and Virgil as soon as she could, but Acropolis Place was—if Kathleen could beg her pardon—"rather out of the way." When Kathleen suggested the old girlfriends meet on campus, a mini reunion, Patricia snorted. Kathleen would barely recognize the place, she said. UD had desegregated—didn't she know?

Kathleen almost hung up on her.

Virgil suggested a trip to campus anyway, "for old times' sake," so they went and showed Nicholas and Nathaniel the Green, where students were reading and bicycling, the Memorial Library, where Mother and Father had met, and where Kathleen was sorry to see her photo still hung. Had there been no Notable Women since '48? They showed the boys Warner Hall, where a girl faced expulsion if her room wasn't clean, and of course the tennis courts, where Mother won the intercollegiate tournament two years in a row.

The boys were tired. They had heard all about the tennis already, they said. The family stopped for ice cream on the way home. Nicholas expressed a desire for bicycles.

All through June and into July the pool remained covered. The mower mowed the grass in the small courtyard but avoided trimming the pool's edges, and as summer bore on, grass grew up around the concrete in a weedy kidney. Kathleen thought she should have known better by the bizarre words their landlord had used to advertise the pool in the pamphlet (*Refreshing! Ecstatic!*), but when she researched temporary homes in the area, Acropolis Place was their lone option. They both pretended that it was Kathy's turn to pick out a place, since Virgil chose Bend Street, but really there was no choice. Virgil had quit his job. The house in Pawtucket sold for what they had paid almost a decade ago. It was what they could afford.

Kathleen supposed she didn't do something about the swimming pool sooner because she'd assumed through the summer that things were, in fact, temporary, that they would find a house in Wilmington by the fall. Then there was the trip to California. So it wasn't until the end of August that she looked out at the covered pool through her sliding glass door and realized they would be living in apartment 14B for much longer than Virgil had promised.

Kathleen did not know what was going on at Equitable Insurance, but she had stopped talking to Virgil about his work a long time ago. Meanwhile the boys, who had campaigned relentlessly over the summer to swim in the pool, gave up their grievances once they returned from California and school started.

Nicholas, who typically enjoyed making up stories, telling tall tales, returned home from the first day of school in love with the truth: he told his mother that he and Nathaniel *hated* Acropolis Place, and they *hated* the pool, and even if the stupid pool opened, they had vowed not to use it on principle. There was a bigger, better pool at their school, he said, and that's where all the other kids swam anyway. The little kidney-shaped pool was for *old people*, Nicholas declared, so that's when Kathleen decided to, at long last, sort out the swimming-pool business.

She went downstairs and tried lifting the cover herself. It was ridiculously heavy. So she went to 1A, to speak with their landlord. When she knocked on the door, Cosmo Parousia Jr. answered promptly.

"Good morning, Mrs. Beckett," he said. "How may I assist you?"

He was born in Thessaloniki in 1918, he had explained to Virgil and Kathleen, as they signed the rental agreement, and lived there for fifteen years before his father made the plan to emigrate with the whole family to New York in '33. Due to a language mix-up, they had ended up departing the Hotel Dixie bus station on 42nd Street on a bus headed for Newark, Delaware.

If the Parousias panicked when they found themselves being driven out of the city, it did not last: on the bus they learned that a sizable Greek population would await them in Newark. In nearby Wilmington, Greek-owned restaurants and confectionaries lined Market Street, above one of which was a Greek language school. Cosmo's father, Cosmo Sr., who had been taught by his own father that any man with a community was a success, quickly nurtured relationships and, before long, was a key figure in the establishment of the 95th Chapter of the American Hellenic Educational Progressive Association in Wilmington. By '39, the association had raised forty thousand dollars to build a Greek Orthodox church, and when the association raised over a hundred thousand in a massive fundraiser held in the Gold Ballroom of the Hotel DuPont—with such dignitaries in attendance as Governor Richard McMullen and Wilmington's mayor, Walter Bacon—Cosmo Parousia Sr. raised a glass of champagne and gave a rousing toast that so impressed Mayor Bacon, next in line for governor, that he personally helped Mr. Parousia purchase a large plot of land on a hill in southwest Newark, upon which he might build housing for young couples of modest means, to give them a head start in life. Cosmo Sr., though he had never studied architecture before, turned to his Euclid, and four years later, Acropolis Place was up and running.

The building, he said, would look Greek. It was three stories high, and constructed with brick and white stucco. Everyone had their own kitchen and fireplace. When Cosmo Sr. retired a decade later at the age of sixty-six, Cosmo Jr., who had served as his father's assistant all those years, took over management of the complex.

It had been his idea to install a swimming pool in the center of the pentagon.

He was now thirty-nine years old, eight years past Kathleen, and sported a white summer shirt and high-waisted white shorts when he opened the door.

Perhaps it was because he was so short that the waist of his shorts sat so high, Kathleen thought. The top of his head just reached her shoulders. Below his neck, an animal tuft of black chest hair exploded from the collar, and she could make out the rest of the hair on his torso in pricking patterns underneath the shirt. Cosmo Jr.'s face, smooth and tan, looked strange, she thought, when you considered the rest of him. How long the man spent shaving each morning, Kathleen did not know, but given what she knew of the headache it was to groom her own body, she respected it.

"Mr. Parousia," she said. "Good morning. I'm sorry to bother you, but I'm wondering why the pool is closed, and what we might do to use it."

"Please. Call me Cosmo," he said, and blinked his long eyelashes.

"Cosmo," said Kathleen.

"Yes," he said. "I'm sorry, but the pool is closed."

"May I ask why?" said Kathleen. She held up the pamphlet and showed him the picture of the pool in the center of the pentagon that had been promised to them.

Cosmo Jr.'s little shoulders crept up to his chin. He closed his eyes and breathed heavily, pressing both palms together as though in prayer, holding the bible of his own hands at his lips. "Two years ago, my father. He was swimming in it, and—I'm sorry to tell you, Mrs. Beckett—he drowned."

Kathleen stepped back from the door. She felt awful. Of *course* there had been a reason the pool was closed.

"Oh my gosh," she said, and touched his arm. "Oh my goodness, Mr. Parousia. I'm so sorry. I had no idea."

"I've thought about opening the pool, but it's taken some time, as you can imagine. No one else has wanted to swim in it. You are the first to ask."

"I understand," said Kathleen. "Don't worry about it. I'm so very sorry."

She turned immediately to leave, but Cosmo stopped her. "Mrs. Beckett," he said. "You're right. It's been too long. Give me a week, please. The pool will be ready."

So it was that during the first week of September, with Virgil at work and the boys back at school, Kathleen had watched from the balcony as a small group of Greek men arrived to clean the swimming pool.

The men, all with shiny black hair like Cosmo's, rather looked the same to Kathleen, and she peripherally wondered if they were all Parousias. Whoever they were, they worked quietly and expediently, shrieking only when they removed the old pool cover, which, when unfolded, revealed a badly molded underbelly. The water beneath had not been drained after the accident, and what remained was a grim-looking lagoon of black and brown leaves. Mysterious, sticky debris rimmed the sides, and the stink of it filled the entire complex for two days.

Cosmo posted a notice to all of his tenants to keep their windows closed.

The pool cleaners brought garden hoses, long scrubbing brushes, and a big metal watering can that appeared to contain some kind of bleach. They spent three days scrubbing until, at last, a white surface of concrete began to appear. When the pool was clean and refilled, Cosmo installed a fresh water filter and arranged the delivery of a brand-new beige pool cover from an outfit in Baltimore. It was ready.

The weekend passed. Kathleen kept glancing outside to see if anyone was swimming, but it was as though the old people had all gotten used to life without the pool and had forgotten about it. Maybe they were still frightened by the drowning of the older Cosmo Parousia and did not trust the water, or maybe they were just troubled by the news out of Little Rock and were too preoccupied to swim, Kathleen did not know, but when even her own boys showed no interest, she felt guilty. It was her fault Cosmo had had to go through all that, and the Becketts really wouldn't be staying all that long at the complex. Fall would be here in under a month.

The cleaning out of the pool must have been, she thought, so very difficult for her landlord and his family, and by Monday afternoon of the following week, Kathleen had troubled herself so deeply about it that she decided to apologize. She returned downstairs and knocked on the door of 1A.

This time it took a few minutes, and when Cosmo opened the door, he appeared as though he had been weeping.

"Come in, Mrs. Beckett," he said.

The apartment smelled like black pepper and cooking oil. From the living room, Kathleen could see into the Parousias' kitchen, where not one but two fat teakettles sat steaming on the stove. A large marble mortar-and-pestle was stationed next to the kettles on the counter. Mrs. Parousia, who did not speak English — "Mama," he called her — was apparently not home, but Kathleen observed that fresh herbs had been recently hung upside down in the window.

"Please, Mrs. Beckett," Cosmo said, sniffling, and gestured to a chair.

She didn't sit down. When she offered to get Cosmo a tissue, or perhaps make him tea, he moaned a little, holding himself.

Kathleen Beckett could not say, in the awkward silence of Cosmo Parousia Jr.'s living room, why she reached behind her neck to undo the clasp of her dress, but as she closed her eyes and unhooked it, she was thinking about Billy Blasko that fall day he came to see her on Bend Street. They had not spoken since. When Cosmo lunged at her, and began to passionately kiss her neck and breasts, when his small hands greedily clutched at Kathleen's hips, they were not his hands, and as he groaned, "Please, Mrs. Beckett," over and over, and stood on his tiptoes, smooching her clavicle, Billy's lips touched her skin. *Walk in the way of love, just as Christ loved us and gave himself up for us as a fragrant offering and sacrifice to God,* Kathleen thought, as Cosmo yanked her zipper down.

9.

Virgil left 14B and descended the stairs to the swimming pool for the last time, trying to figure out how to explain the phone call to Kathleen. She already didn't like his father, and he couldn't imagine she even cared all that much what happened to him—it was not so bad, Virgil told himself, that she didn't care at *all*—but Coke Beckett's stories were usually about something that had happened a long time ago. Virgil was beginning to gently mull over the possibility, however outlandish, of what Coke had said, when he reached the landing, turned the corner, and saw, in the blue-black light of early evening, Cosmo

Parousia Jr. sitting next to his wife at the edge of the swimming pool.

His landlord's legs were sticking out straight, crossed at the ankles, and he was leaning back on two hands, staring up at the darkening sky as though the sun were still shining. They looked like a couple, Virgil thought, both in midlife and long in love: Kathleen, a tall, thick-legged, college-educated former athlete leaning her back against one side of a swimming pool, with Cosmo, a short, hairy landlord from some town in Greece no one had ever heard of, positioned next to her in a way that signaled eternal commitment. There was not enough space between them to make Virgil feel easy about what he saw, but he couldn't seriously entertain the idea. What was it Kathleen called him? *The Little Troll.*

"Mr. Parousia," he said, and worked himself into a smile. "Maybe you can help. Looks like someone won't get out of the pool."

Cosmo grinned. "I'm very glad people are swimming," he said, waving a flat hand at the water. "Nobody ever uses this pool, and it's a lot of work to keep it. I'm glad people are using it."

It's not "people," Virgil thought, *it's my wife,* and turned to face her. "Kathy," he said. "Honey, you must be freezing. Are you feeling okay?"

She stared at the water. "I'm perfectly fine," she said.

Virgil straightened himself. "Well, what do you want to do for dinner? The boys are ready."

Kathleen lifted a watery hand toward their balcony.

"There's a Chicken Cordon Bleu in the fridge. Thirty minutes at three fifty. I'll be up shortly," she said.

"Kathleen," Virgil said. "My God, look at your fingers."

Mrs. Beckett looked at her swollen hands. They'd papered. Around her fingernails, the puckered skin had long ago begun to slough, shredding her cuticles.

"I know," she said. "Isn't that funny?"

Cosmo stood up and stretched. "Time to go. Good evening, Kathleen," he said. "Virgil."

If he had given it any thought, Virgil might have realized that it was the first time the landlord had addressed them by their Christian names, and not "Mr. and Mrs. Beckett," and aside from between the giggles of young nurses in Naples who called him *"Il Poeta,"* Virgil had never heard his name spoken by a foreign tongue before. As Cosmo walked past him, Virgil felt a disturbance he could not articulate: the top of the man's shoulder ever so slightly pressured one of Virgil's right biceps. It was just aggressive enough to make Virgil turn away from Kathleen and watch the little landlord waddle his way through the front door of 1A.

"Kathy," Virgil said, "get serious, will you? It's time to get out."

"Not yet," she said.

Virgil listened to the evening air and heard a crazy, high-pitched laugh. The geese were gone. "You should have heard Coke on the phone. You know, I think he really might be losing it."

"What did he say?"

"He wanted to know your blood type. He was making no sense. Doesn't sound well at all."

Kathleen shoved her body away from him into the center of the pool. A dark, wet leaf attached itself to one of her shoulders. She dunked her head underwater and surfaced, smoothing her hair with both hands. "I almost forgot," she said. "There was another call today. A woman."

"Who was it?" he said.

"She didn't say who she was. She said she was looking for someone called 'Charlie.'"

Above them, Mrs. Donovan's silhouette shifted into, and out from, her curtains.

"A wrong number, it sounds like," he said.

(Was that his voice?)

"She wanted to know if 'Charlie' got it,'" Kathleen said, and for the first time all day, it seemed, looked at his face. "What did you get?"

Everyone was waiting. The boys, for their dinner. Mrs. Donovan was waiting, but not for Kathleen; she, too, was worried about her dinner. Would they feed her, gadding about the pool all day, or would she have to settle for leftovers?

It was Sunday. Coke was waiting for his son to call him back, Artie Wooz was waiting for Louis Porter to die, Tom Braddock was waiting to get out of Wilmington, and Little Mo, surprised that Virgil hadn't called by now, had somehow tracked down his new number and called instead. She was waiting to hear if he got the saxophone. And now Kathleen was waiting for Virgil to answer.

God only knew what Little Mo had said to her.

Virgil's mouth opened. All he needed to find were two words—"a saxophone"—then it could begin, it could all start right here, by this cheap community swimming pool, he thought, as the weight of his body bore down through his golf shoes onto the concrete. He could feel his own gravity as the November moon crested the roof.

It was still warm out, but the air smelled like cold water. White lights from the televisions in people's green living rooms flickered and glowed, making the pentagon look like some kind of spaceship, and Virgil half expected the entire complex of Acropolis Place to rip itself from the earth, hover briefly, then begin its ascent. A *dog* was up there now, he thought dizzily, flying right over his head, and it was as though everything he once trusted as logical was illogical. The definitions of dream and reality as he had long understood them were inverted: dream was the reasoning conducted by principles of validity, and reality was all that was unreasonable. Invalid. He was headed toward something totally strange, he knew, as his mind raced through a series of inadequate answers: "A saxophone, I don't know who from" or "Someone sent me a saxophone" or "A client bought me a saxophone." It all sounded awful, almost worse than the truth.

What did he get, Kathleen wanted to know, but Virgil didn't know what he got. An instrument he could not play.

The new house he had promised Kathleen was still so far off, and the way things were going at Equitable, if he were completely honest about it, they wouldn't be able to leave Acropolis Place until spring. Maybe summer. Maybe longer. Virgil worked on commission now, and had not signed one single new client. The Bluebird was his on *advance*. A motivational tool, he was told by Lou Porter, and he already owed the company back payments.

People liked him, and the look of the new robin's-egg car, they were happy to speak with him—Virgil Beckett was so *awfully* nice to look at—but when it came time to sign, commit their money, they always backed off. Virgil didn't get it. He had done everything right. Over the past six months, he quit drinking, quit women. He was going to church.

Artie Wooz still believed in him—it was impossible not to *want* to believe in Virgil Beckett—but last week had warned him that he might be in trouble at Equitable if he couldn't make any business. He told Virgil to be more persistent, "call *every day* if you have to," and just this afternoon, as they parted ways, Wooz winked at him and said, "Use *Sputnik*." The man himself had a recording of the steady beeping sound *Sputnik 1* made, which he played for housewives in their living rooms. In front of their children. "Be kind. Take your time," Wooz said. "Tell them they have a beautiful home, beautiful children, but *there is no security in beauty*" —

Artie Wooz, he thought, disgusted. Artie Wooz was a *jackass*. The whole insurance business was full of *jackasses*, and at that moment Virgil Beckett experienced for the first time the sobriety he thought he'd already achieved: What in the *hell* was he doing back in Newark? Acropolis Place? The apartments had been built on a hill, like the Acropolis of Athens, the Acropolis of Rhodes, but this wasn't Greece. It was Delaware.

The day before Virgil left Italy, he had visited the Duomo di Napoli, the cathedral in Naples that had miraculously survived both war and volcano, and that the nurses insisted he see. Virgil had never seen a cathedral before. When he hobbled up the stone steps on his crutches, passed through the facade, he was stunned by the tremendous scale of it all, the cold smell of limestone, the intricate frescoes, massive bronze statues, the light pouring in through the windows of the apse, pulling him toward an incandescent white and gold sculpture of the assumption of Mary at Ephesus, a woman being taken up, body and soul, into heaven. The place was empty except for a row of Neapolitans offering quiet prayers at her feet, and Virgil knew at once that he could not stay. He didn't even go to church. The Italians and their cathedral, their dream of Mary, it was something real, and he, Virgil Beckett, crutching quickly out of the Duomo, was a fake. Kathleen—carefully observing him from her place in the swimming pool—had always called him a faker. Right from the start. He could just ditch it all, he thought, all of this fake life, and move west, back home. Clearly his father, more than ever, needed him now—

It was so simple. He could go back. The saxophone was in the trunk of the Bluebird, and it was three hundred twelve miles to Pawtucket. Virgil could say "a saxophone" to Kathleen and then it would happen: he would have it out with his wife, then leave the state, abscond with the Bluebird up to Crooly's and surprise Little Mo. He would take the redheaded cock-tail waitress and the saxophone to the Lincoln Highway across Pennsylvania, through the Midwest, to Salt Lake City, and then over to Reno. Virgil had just done the whole drive, and could do it again from memory. The boys would get interesting postcards. He would arrive at Coke's cabin in Big Sur with pretty little Imogene Monson on his arm, and she could take care of his father. Coke would like Imogene. The girl was brutally honest, and swore like a teenager.

Virgil already knew how to wrap his whole body around her.

Weekends they could take the Bluebird to Monterey, could hit the Golden State Theatre, and he would tell her, over and over, about having seen Charlie Parker there once. As for Sundays? *Fuck* golf. Sundays could be his once again: free, long, sun-dunked days at Del Monte Beach like when Virgil was young: laying out a blanket on the broad, flat sand to watch the rows of surfers paddle up glassy waves before cresting, popping up on their heels, disappearing into great barrels of white water to then either emerge from the other end fast and unscathed, or tumble painfully into the break. Little Mo, all smiles, would show off a high-waisted bikini with a strapless, ruffled top. Cherry-red lipstick. She would carry a picnic basket and go barefoot in the sand. Virgil, holding her hand, would wear a long-sleeved double-breasted chamois with the sleeves rolled up. Sunglasses. Saddle shoes. No socks. He'd always worn shoes on the beach.

The saxophone. He could learn how to play it at last, and imagined himself sitting on the picnic table outside Coke's cabin after his father died, blowing "All the Things You Are" into the sea.

The moon was positioning itself over the swimming pool. This warm day in November, it would not last. It was coming to an end. The first vacant chill of night reached under Virgil's clothes, touching his skin. Tomorrow, it would be cold again. On Friday, he and Kathleen had plans to go into Wilmington. They were supposed to go see *Jailhouse Rock*. Would they? The *saxophone*, he thought, and Virgil moved the word around in his mouth until it nearly spilled out — Kathleen was looking at him now very intently — but the word wasn't there. What was a saxophone? The thing in the trunk of the Bluebird, the Jolly Frank, with its absurd rooster logo? The saxophone was J-shaped and complicated, a perplexing mess of vents and levers, pins and rollers, the gold and mother-of-pearl buttons that ran the length of the instrument — keys, right? They were called keys? Some of them already seemed to stick. On his tongue, the bitter taste of the reed still lingered. The saxophone was an entire language Virgil Beckett would have to learn — but how exhausting!

Why had Little Mo given him the saxophone? Really, it was a pretty destructive thing to do, he thought, to send it to his office like that. What other destruction might Little Mo bring? The girl was just twenty-one. Kathleen had always said her parents fought because her mother was too young for her father. Little Mo would grow up, want children. Her figure, a tiny trunk and all legs, would not recover well — certainly not as well as Kathleen, who was tall — and Little Mo drank. A *lot*. She might like living with him at the cabin in Big Sur — or not. There she would stand, round, ruddy-cheeked, and hot-tempered in Coke's tiny kitchen, refusing to do the dishes because there was no proper sink. She wasn't *from* here, she'd shout, throwing a plate against the wall; she wanted to *get out of here, get out of California*, and he would—at the age of what, forty?—begin the long decades that would ensue ignoring her. Little Mo was risky. And Virgil Beckett did not take risks.

He closed his eyes and saw his mother tossing her pretty blond head in the air, walking down Del Monte Avenue in a peach chiffon dress:

It's a *perfect* morning in Monterey. The sun is out. Inland, back from the bay, oranges growing in orchards and stock farms fill the sea air. Bitsy Beckett glances at a crying seagull, then watches the newsboys unloading bricks of papers, which land at their feet with a thud. But look there, just yonder! The Japanese abalone divers across the street are rescuing one of their men, who nearly drowned trying to loosen the sucker of a plate-sized red lip shell. How sad, she thinks, as she steps off the curb, into the street. Her instinct, born from the earthquake, is to move toward tragedy, not away from it. She's not afraid. She might be able to help, she thinks. It's something in the way they are carrying that man out of the water by his arms and legs like he's a table, laying him down on the grass in his diving suit, removing the large round diving helmet to attempt resuscitation. Is he breathing? Poor thing! It's impossible to see…

The bus had come for Virgil now. He had not looked where he was going. He would never learn to play the saxophone. He hadn't even made it to New York. He'd gone to Delaware.

He hadn't even *studied* music in college. His major had been psychology.

"Don't play the saxophone, let it play you," Charlie Parker said, and Virgil realized, with a start, that it was exactly what he'd done.

He was almost there now, he'd almost decided, but he could not speak yet: Kathleen was in charge. She already knew he was "Charlie." All those weeknights he had come home drunk, reeking of smoke and perfume. She knew it all. He'd grown terribly lazy over the years. Breath mints, earrings. Matchbooks with phone numbers left in his pockets. Once, a whole tube of red lipstick. It was all so open, so cliché, so obvious and indiscreet, you could have argued that it was as though he'd *wanted* his wife to notice, and say something. She never said anything. A saxophone. Kathy must *want* him to tell her the truth, he considered, otherwise why bother to mention the call from the woman at all? If he could just speak the words and confess, maybe it wouldn't ruin his marriage; maybe his wife was offering him this chance to clear the air. So she might forgive him. Or would she divorce him?

Virgil knew he was trapped: the past had to make itself known. He had to go back, only then could he move forward. This marriage—or what they pretended about it—had to die. It was time. Virgil would tell her everything, and not just about Little Mo and the saxophone—all the girls. It was long overdue. He didn't know what would happen, but he was ready.

He was in the wrong, so Kathleen couldn't directly confront him; he had to be the one to start. *A saxophone*, he thought

again, and almost said it as the moon over the roof of the pentagon, bright and gibbous, lit up the pool water, turning the air a
dull gray. Death was imminent, but Virgil wasn't afraid.

In 1937, on the Golden Gate Bridge, a man dressed in a
fine, tailored black suit had lingered near him and Bitsy, listening to his mother as she sang, *"Silvery charms caress the arms
I'm longing for."* The man looked young, but his temples were
white. He was missing his hat. He had stood at the railing with
them, and when Bitsy waited for the cars to pass and crossed
the bridge to the other side, pulling Virgil with her, the man followed them. He removed his jacket, his vest. He declared himself a veteran of the Great War, shouted, "You can't go back,"
then ascended the four-foot-high railing, blew Bitsy a kiss, and
stepped off the edge, sending his body whistling to the water
below. How strange it was that Virgil was only remembering
him now. Did it even happen?

Kathleen was still waiting. Cold water ebbed from her
round shoulders, lit by the moon in silver rings. The wet drape
of dark hair on her head looked like a helmet. Virgil's heart was
light. He loved Kathleen. He really did. He loved the boys.

"A saxophone," he said, and fell, fully clothed, into the
swimming pool.

10.

How small Virgil looked to Kathleen as he walked upstairs to call his father, golf bag in tow. How strange it was, she thought, that every Sunday her husband wanted to play a game he never won. She had never understood it. Kathleen shivered, rubbing her feet together in the pool. She had a few more laps in her. She could feel the skin on her heels peeling off into water as she watched Virgil pace between the kitchen and living room, talking to his father on the phone. She did not have to guess what Coke was telling him.

In the summer of 1950, a year after Nathaniel was born,

Coke had driven across the country, uninvited, to see the baby. Kathleen was four months pregnant with Nicholas. The afternoon he arrived at Bend Street, she and Virgil had been genuinely astonished to see him. They led him inside the house, right upstairs to the nursery, and Coke stood over the crib with a frown. "He looks nothing like you," he said, and Virgil replied, "What are you talking about—of course he does," but Coke shook his head. "*No*," he said, louder. "The baby always looks like the father, and *this one doesn't*."

Nathaniel started to cry. Virgil quickly ushered his father out of the nursery, and Kathleen followed behind them, nervously, on the stairs. She went into the kitchen and listened while the two of them argued in the living room. Coke was shouting about the books she kept on her bookshelf. He pulled down one of Billy's novels, and Kathleen heard him throw it on the coffee table. "What in the hell is this?" he said. "Your *mother* read magazines!"

Kathleen heard Virgil come, in his way, to her defense: "She *doesn't* read them," he said. "Look, they're all dog-eared!"

But Coke said that was worse. What was his wife doing keeping a bunch of books she never finished? "I don't trust her," he said, and because Colson Beckett was the sort of man who believed his opinion was so good it was always worth repeating, he said: "No, I do *not*."

Colson and Kathleen had managed to tolerate each other for these nine long years, but only because they never saw each other. Only once in all that time did Kathleen think she might say something irreparable.

This past August, after Coke had complained to Virgil about chest palpitations (as though anything, she'd thought, could palpitate in that steely, rusted heart), they'd packed up their new Bluebird and driven themselves all that way across the Lincoln Highway. Kathleen sent their friends postcards. When they arrived in Big Sur, they discovered that the cabin on the coast had only one bedroom, which Coke kept for himself. Kathleen and Virgil were on folding cots in the living room that Coke had salvaged someplace, and the boys camped out back in sleeping bags, by Coke's picnic table in a small, rocky yard that had a sprawling ocean view.

The cabin, a lopsided horizontal shanty with a thatched roof swarming with ivy, had been built by some of the earliest settlers to the area, Coke said satisfactorily, men who really knew what it meant to live off the land. There was a small fireplace but no other heat source. The plumbing had been jerry-rigged using an old wine barrel Coke had turned into a rainwater cistern. During dry spells, well — you were clean out of luck, he said.

The eighth night in, Kathleen, sick and exhausted from the constant smoke inhalation, from staying up late yet again listening to Virgil's father tell obscene stories, had not slept well. At first light, she gave up trying. She rose from her cot to make the coffee, when she heard a muffled whimper from Coke's bedroom.

It would be so like him, she thought, to be keeping a dog they'd never met.

It was a raw, black morning on the high coast of California. Outside the cabin, all along the vista, big waves slammed the shore. Kathleen, worried about the boys, went to the backyard and unzipped the tent. Nicholas was asleep, but Nathaniel's sleeping bag was empty. Kathleen thought he might be off somewhere for a pee—the boys, at least, loved doing it outside, in nature—and she walked around the side of the cabin, looking for him. When she saw a light on in Coke's bedroom window, she looked inside.

The man, sixty-one and white-haired, was sitting upright on his bed with Nathaniel sitting next to him. The boy's back was bent at an odd angle in his pajamas, and he was staring, pinch-faced, at the far wall. One of Coke's hands was holding Nathaniel's pajama sleeve, which had been rolled up to his shoulder, and a rubber hose was tightly tied around his arm.

Coke was in the process of injecting a syringe into the soft part of his elbow. "This is called the *cubital fossa*," he said. "And here, this is your median vein."

Kathleen kept watching until the needle was out, then rapped hard on the window. "What do you think you're doing?" she shouted.

Coke rolled Nathaniel's sleeve back down and patted his leg. "Now go back to bed," he said, and did not regard Kathleen at all as he placed the syringe into what appeared to be an ancient medical bag, then stood up, drawing the window curtain across her face.

Kathleen insisted that the family pack up and leave that morning. When Virgil asked why, she simply said she couldn't go on without a proper bathroom. Nathaniel had barely spoken the whole ride home and hadn't said much since. Now he preferred to let Nicholas do the talking for him. She worried about her son's silence, and didn't know whether he realized anything had happened to him, but Kathleen knew that now, like it or not, from the swimming pool at Acropolis Place Apartments with the November sky pinking dark above her, dried leaves blowing endlessly into her pool, things were about to change. It was getting cold. It wouldn't be long before she would have to get out, but she would stay in for as long as it took.

In 1948, a mere two months after Kathleen had won her second and last intercollegiate tennis championship at UD and moved to Pawtucket, she read in the paper that Margaret Osborne duPont had beat a fierce Oklahoma backhander, Louise Brough, 15–13 after forty-eight games. It was the longest female tennis final ever recorded. Kathleen couldn't bear it, what she had become. So she would become someone else. She went upstairs and put her trench coat on over her nightgown. Messed up her hair. Slid on her makeup all wrong. She had quit tennis too easily, she knew, and was angry at herself for letting a person like Randy Roman operate on her confidence. Four years later, in '52, Kathleen read in the paper that Margaret had given birth to a son. Two years after that, she won Wimbledon. Again. She'd already won it four times.

DuPont, Kathleen laughed to herself in the pool. It meant "from the bridge." Billy was only partially right about tennis; it was about posture, movement, but it was mainly about endurance. That's all she needed now. With a little extra endurance, it would all soon be over. Kathleen Lovelace, the president of the University of Delaware told her, had such *remarkable* endurance. So did Kathleen Beckett. She adjusted the straps of her bathing suit and lifted her arms into the air, stretching.

A scoop of light appeared outside apartment 1A. Nicholas and Nathaniel sprinted out from the Parousias' and made for the staircase.

Kathleen and Cosmo had only spoken pleasantries to each other since that morning in September, but with Virgil upstairs, Kathleen watched him open the door and follow behind the boys, walking out, in his waddling way, to the pool.

He handed her a glass of water like he understood what she was doing.

"Do you need anything else?" he said.

"No, thank you," she said, and turned off the radio.

Cosmo sat down next to her, on the concrete. He extended his legs and leaned back on both hands. He gazed at the sky. "They sent up another one," he said.

"I know," said Kathleen. "They sent a dog up this time."

"Yes," Cosmo said.

"She's going to die," said Kathleen, and she could tell that Cosmo wanted to say something else. She was glad that he didn't. The way he had stationed his body so close to hers by the pool, however, was unacceptable. "You should go back inside," she said.

"I'm worried about you," he said.

"I'm fine," she said. "Don't worry about me at all."

Cosmo tilted back his head as the last slice of sun moved

over the roof of the pentagon and the heavens appeared, black and blue. He said what he wanted to say:

"He does not deserve you."

"Yes, he does," Kathleen said, and that was all before Virgil's shadow descended, turned the corner from the staircase, and walked toward the pool.

"*Kathy*," he said. "Honey, you must be freezing. Are you feeling okay?"

She stared at the water. "I'm perfectly fine," she said.

Virgil straightened himself. "Well, what do you want to do for dinner? The boys are ready."

Kathleen lifted a watery hand toward their balcony. "There's a Chicken Cordon Bleu in the fridge. Thirty minutes at three fifty. I'll be up shortly," she said.

"Kathleen," Virgil said. "My God, look at your fingers."

She looked at her hands. "I know," she said. "Isn't that funny?"

Cosmo stood up and stretched. "Time to go. Good evening, Kathleen," he said. "Virgil."

The Becketts both watched their landlord walk back into his apartment. The light outside 1A was turned off.

"Kathy," Virgil said, "get serious, will you? It's time to get out."

But Kathleen was not ready to get out of the pool. Once she got out, everything would go back to normal, and normal was no longer acceptable. She did not know when she got up this morning that today would be the day, but so it was. Virgil had talked to Coke. She knew she would have to tell him about the past, but she had not yet decided whether to tell him about the future. Kathleen Beckett would remain in the swimming pool, weightless, for as long as she had to be. "Not yet," she said.

It would have to come from Virgil first. Because she was also in the wrong. Only by him first telling her about the girl on the phone might he, in turn, forgive her. From the middle of the pool, Kathleen watched Mrs. Donovan's silhouette move into, and out from, her curtains before she braced herself, dunking her head underwater one last time, and surfacing, smoothing her hair with both hands.

"I almost forgot," she said. "There was another call today. A woman."

"Who was it?" said Virgil.

"She didn't say who she was. She said she was looking for someone called 'Charlie.'"

"A wrong number, it sounds like," Virgil said.

And there it was: the serve, the volley. For the first time all day, Kathleen looked at her husband. He was truly *so* beautiful. She felt sorry for him. "She wanted to know if 'Charlie' got it," she said. "What did you get?"

The lights of the living rooms at Acropolis Place all began switching on, glowing. The stars, if they were shining, were quite invisible. Kathleen had married Virgil Beckett precisely because he wasn't like any other boy she ever knew—and because he was exactly what she, as a young girl, had wanted a husband to be. Unlike her parents, Virgil barely ever raised his voice, not even to Nicholas. Whether here or in Pawtucket, he was tranquil. When he smiled, he showed all of his teeth.

He wasn't competitive. He didn't like change. He liked to lie down, listen to jazz. Bebop. His hair, the color of sunshine, grew lighter in summer, and he still combed it the same way every day, with his father's old buffalo comb. This move back to Delaware, this going to church business—she knew he was kidding himself. From the doors of the First Presbyterian, after the services ended, Kathleen saw Virgil's unease in the suit he wore, in the way he talked to the other men he now worked with at Equitable. It was clear to Kathleen, if no one else, that Virgil didn't fit in. But she had never wanted him to.

She could blame Billy Blasko—ever since Billy, Kathleen had found the company of American men either comical or intolerable. In college, many times over, she had heard them say vile things to one another about women, but Virgil Beckett had done none of that. He didn't know he was supposed to. He, too, was an outsider, the rare West Coaster who, for some reason, had found his way east. Time itself had always seemed to pass gently in Virgil's company, and as Kathleen stared at him, slowly drawing her husband, in her way, onto the bridge, watching him turn over in his mind what she had offered him—a chance to tell her the truth so that she might, too, tell him the truth—tonight was no different. There they were, suspended.

She had not planned it. The moment had arrived in its due course, and in the dark swimming pool, Kathleen Beckett began shaking. If her life with Virgil up to now was some unrecoverable lie, then all of her memories were lies too. She no longer played tennis. That dream was done. If Virgil insisted that he had nothing to confess? So be it.

Regardless, seven months from now, there would be a new, fat, black-haired baby girl who would suffer a lifetime struggling to manage a stubborn Greek mustache.

All Virgil needed to do was tell her what the woman gave him, and it could begin, so she waited. Kathleen Beckett could wait a long time. She was freezing cold, yet felt in the water that her body was terribly strong—but it was up to Virgil now.

Above them, in outer space, a little Moscow street dog was crying out in her chamber. She was far from where she had been picked up, by the fountain in Sokolniki Park. The harness she wore was too tight. The tiny capsule into which she had been placed was losing oxygen. It beeped and shook. The heat shield had failed; it was over a hundred degrees. Her pulse was decreasing. Death was imminent. Mrs. Donovan and all the other old folks, in singles and pairs, had come to Acropolis Place to die. Though she hardly knew anything about him, Kathleen imagined Cosmo Sr. standing where she was now, in the center of the pool, suffering his malady, a heart attack, helplessly taking in mouthfuls of water, and Kathleen had seen in her own body all day the dip and float of the dead Greek man. That Braddock boy had died a month ago. Kathleen had heard that Sally, the boy's mother, whom Kathleen had often seen at church but never spoken to, was living a dream, pretending it had never happened, pretending that her eldest son was enrolled at UD. She was telling her friends, brightly, that he was studying physics and had laughed off Reverend Underhill's request for the funeral arrangements. Her husband, Tom, had already filed for divorce.

All around them was death, and Kathleen had never been more in love with Virgil in her life. The way he was standing there in the dark in those silly golf clothes, those black-and-white wingtips, trying all day—and failing—to get his wife out of the pool. Oh, how he was *trying*. But Virgil did not have Kathleen's endurance.

He was on the bridge now. Kathleen knew her opponent well. She had her husband locked in the volley and was drawing him closer. He had no idea what was about to happen, but time was running out, the fuse was lit.

It was going to hurt; nobody said it wouldn't. But even if "Charlie Parker" had slept with every woman on the eastern seaboard, it hardly mattered to Kathleen. She would be honest with him as soon as he would do the same. All they needed was a little death. Nine years of a marriage was *nothing*, when you thought about it. People went sixty years, sometimes longer. She would let him get it all out, and when he was finished telling her the truth about the man he wanted to be, but wasn't, she could tell him the truth about the woman she was. Wanted to be. Kathleen was prepared to tell him everything.

Acknowledgments

I am overwhelmingly grateful and lucky for Jean Garnett, who has twice now gifted me with her truly extraordinary editorial vision, and I also wish to thank the inimitable Betsy Uhrig and the entire team at Little, Brown for all of their hard work shepherding this story into the world with such care. Jim Rutman, too, must be thanked here, as I am always indebted to him for his deep patience and his uncanny way of knowing precisely when a time is right. This novel was born in Štúrovo, Slovakia, and so I thank Karol Frühauf for selecting me as the forty-first Bridge Guard of the Mária Valéria Bridge. I also thank Kirsty Dunseath at Penguin Random House UK and those readers here in the States who helped me to realize this work in more ways than I can name: Kate Christensen, Jason Ockert, Brian Brodeur, Thomas Israel Hopkins, Tracy Zeman, Amy Amoroso, my dear parents, Tom and Sue Anthony, and in the final hour, my sister Julie. Finally, my biggest thanks and love are for my partner, Jon, who fulfills every definition of that word.

About the Author

Jessica Anthony is the author of three books of fiction, most recently the novel *Enter the Aardvark*, a finalist for the New England Book Award in Fiction. Anthony's novels have been published in over a dozen countries and featured in *Time*, *Newsweek*, *The Guardian*, the *Wall Street Journal*, and the *New York Times Book Review* as an Editors' Choice. A recipient of the Creative Capital Award in Literature, Anthony has also received support from the Bogliasco Foundation in Italy, MacDowell, the Bridge Guard Foundation, and the Maine Arts Commission. She recently spent a month in residence at the Fred W. Smith National Library for the Study of George Washington.